*Also by Jayne Loader:*

BETWEEN PICTURES

# WILD AMERICA

## Jayne Loader

IVY BOOKS • NEW YORK

Ivy Books
Published by Ballantine Books
Copyright © 1989 by Jayne Loader

Library of Congress Catalog Card Number: 88-26073

ISBN 0-8041-0644-4

This edition published by arrangement with Grove Press, a Division of Wheatland Corporation

Manufactured in the United States of America

First Ballantine Books Edition: August 1990

Cover painting detail of "The Traveler" predella 1982, by
Christian Couture

*for Eric*

# Contents

I Was a Hollywood Sex Slave
by Carrie Jo Starkweather     1

The Animal in Her     9

Famous Last Words     17

Saturday in the Barn     51

Wild America     63

Ken Kesey Day     81

Song of the Fucked Duck     116

Mr. and Mrs. Skeritt     119

Baldwin County     133

For Artists Only     147

Found in a Trunk in Springfield, Ohio     173

Kismet     196

# I Was a Hollywood Sex Slave
## by Carrie Jo Starkweather

This is my True Confession I write for you to print in your magazine. Please send the money now. Please send it to Mrs. Carrie Jo Starkweather, P.O. Box 309, Kearney, Nebraska. Do not send it to the farm under any circumstances whatsoever because my husband does not know about this True Confession. He thinks I was at my brother's in Humboldt County while we were separated last summer and these true events took place. He thinks the top grade sinsemilla I brought back with me come from there instead of where it actually come from. Do not let him know the awful truth for the sake of his health and mine. DeWitt is VERY JEALOUS. He is a Vietnam vet and a member of the Aryan Nation. He joined in prison where he went for bombing those school buses though I am not supposed to say none of this out loud. I don't know where all the guns come from nor the money neither, that is not part of this True Confession, he don't give me none of it anyway. He practices surviving with his "brothers" twice a month and this is why I need the money: everything gets worse in the winter. When you print this change my name to whatever you want but make out the check the way it says here. I lied to him when we reconciled but now "the truth will out."

Yes it is true. Yes all of it every word I swear. It happened just like I will say, improbable as it may seem for "truth is stranger than fiction." Here goes:

Well when I left the farm I did not know where to go. I thought I would go to Omaha but I did not know nobody there and DeWitt would find me soon enough it is not that far so I called my brother Roger in Humboldt County. But he would not send the money. He said I should make it up with DeWitt, nothing could be as bad as that and if I wanted to come to California I would have to hitchhike like I did the summer after high school tho that was thirty pounds ago or maybe forty by now, "Fess up Carrie." He said it might not be so easy now getting those good long rides or finding places to stay for free in California though his boss Steve was always asking after me. And Steve came in the room while we were talking and told Roger to tell me Hi. Then Roger bet me an ounce of smoke I would not come as I was chicken. HE LAUGHED!! Well this made me so mad I stuck out my thumb because I am not fat only healthy like an Aryan woman should be, DeWitt's Ideal he says. Like a German princess. And nothing happened between me and Steve anyway, only in Roger's head.

Well right away I got a ride with a man of the Jewish persuasion tho I did not know this when I got into the car or I would not have gotten in even tho it was a pink Caddy. His hands were covered with diamond rings. His name was Mr. Cohen OR SO HE SAID.

Well Mr. Cohen he said how far you going little girl and I said all the way to California I'm sick of goddam wheatfields. He said I will take you if you will stop at the next motel and "spend the night" with me. He said I usually do not do this sort of thing I am married but your so pretty I just can't help myself. I said let me out of this "sinmobile" right now I never heard of such nastiness in all my life what kind of woman do you take me for? He said your right I am sorry I am so ashamed I do not know what come over me, the devil must of made me do it he said, and that did not surprise me, it only proved what DeWitt is always saying: The "chosen people"? CHOSEN BY WHO? Then Mr. Cohen said I will take you to Las Vegas where I am going and then because you are such a good girl I will put you on a plane free of charge so you will not have to hitchhike no more it is not safe for a woman alone. So we drove for two days and he did not try to touch me, "we only talked." And in all those motels we had separate bedrooms.

Well when we got to Las Vegas I said I changed my mind I do not want to go to Humboldt County I want to go to Hollywood. He laughed and said perhaps you will be a movie star your pretty enough and I said oh go on I am too old I am thirty. He said Carrie Jo Starkweather I don't believe it you don't look a day over seventeen. He said anyway go to Schwab's drugstore where Lana Turner was discovered and give it a try for me. I said all right I will try it. He took me to the airport and paid for my ticket with his American Express card, "Don't leave home without it." I did not have to do a thing to get the ticket, only talk. When I left I only kissed him once, that was it, we did not do nothing wrong. So I do not know if it's true what they say about Jewish men, he was old enough to be my father and anyway he never took his socks off.

Well I thought I would go to Hollywood so I told the cab driver to take me to Schwab's drugstore on the corner of Hollywood and Vine. I had a New Coke. Mr. Schwab said I did not have to pay but I did, it is wrong to take food from strangers. Then Mr. Tom Cruise he came in and sat down next to me. He said your so pretty are you in pictures? I said no but I would like to be. He said come with me I will get you a screen test because I am Mr. Tom Cruise the star of *Top Gun* and I said oh yes I recognized you right away.

Well so we went to his house and it was awful fine just like in the magazines. Tom said I love you Carrie Jo you are prettier than Miss Kelly McGillis the co-star of *Top Gun*. He got out a bowl of cocaine and said would you like a little sniff? And I said no, oh no never, none for me thank you, I'll "just say no." But Tom he said don't be a square, Carrie, everybody does it in Hollywood, so I did it too and then everything went black I became a coke fiend after just one sniff. It was not my fault, I could not resist. He had a round water bed with plastic goldfish swimming and on it I became A Hollywood Sex Slave though I did not know this at the time. I thought I would be the girlfriend of Mr. Tom Cruise the star of *Top Gun* who said he loved me.

Well then the days passed one much like the rest and I did more "snow" and Mr. Tom Cruise used my body but I was not responsible and he never said he loved me but that he loved Princess Stephanie of Monaco and tho she was romantically linked with Mr. Rob Lowe, Tom said she would never marry a commoner. He did not get me a screen test like he promised. And one night he said I have a friend coming over I want you to "be nice" to him you know what I mean Carrie. I said no I DO NOT know what you mean but Mr. Tom Cruise left and locked the door of the bedroom where I was A Hollywood Sex Slave and I tried to escape but could not, I was too weak from all the drugs. I cried many bitter tears and later I heard someone come into the bedroom and he said do not be afraid Carrie Jo I'll be kind to you I promise and if you are a good girl I will help you escape from here, I am not like Tom. And he was very sweet and did not force me to abuse any more substances and when the sun come up I saw that it was Mr. Don Johnson the star of *Miami Vice*, but he did not help me escape like he promised. Instead he moved into our luxury Beverly Hills mansion just down the hall from the bedroom I shared with Mr. Tom Cruise and tho we still watched *Miami Vice* on Friday it was all reruns, Don was on vacation. Tom would spend the night with me then go to work making movies and leave Don the days until I got quite sore and tired and longed for DeWitt who never used me so hard who often never used me at all since I was not submissive like a good wife should be, I did not make his word my law but complained about how he only watched the TV never me and never listened or talked to me but only to the other men his "brothers." I even bought a vibrator at one of those parties the girls give like Tupperware but it is really "sexware." I wasn't sure what to do but one night I tried it out anyway. DeWitt had drunk so much beer I thought he would not wake up but he did, it ran on batteries and boy did we have us a time that night. But the next day he threw it away.

Well one day Mr. Don Johnson didn't come in the way he usually did after Tom had gone to the studio to act in pictures so I went down the hall and opened the door to Don's bedroom and what did I see but him and Mr. Philip Michael Thomas the co-star of *Miami Vice* locked in a lewd and lascivious embrace. I did not look at what was going on, but I knew it was wrong, against Scripture. Crockett and Tubbs would never do it, and if God had meant it to happen he would have made Adam and Steve though DeWitt told me it often goes on in prisons and in "Sin Francisco" where there are no real women, only Lesbianese and bra-burners. But I was right down the hall.

Well Don he saw me and gasped oh do not tell anybody this will ruin our careers, and I promised not to but I lied, I am telling now, I'm sorry Don, I need the money. And Don he come out to the deluxe sunken living room and sat with me in the conversation pit in front of the genuine wood-burning fireplace. And Philip come out too. They both had on chiffon negligees. Don's was blue, he was the man, and Philip's was pink trimmed with sateen ribbons. Their toenail polish matched their negligees tho you do not see this on *Miami Vice*, they wear shoes. Well in a few minutes Philip went back into the bedroom and came out again and he was not Philip any more he was Mr. Michael Jackson, he wore a red leather jacket and a glove. And Don he said you see now Carrie Jo why I have to take good care of him he has many personalities like in *The Three Faces of Eve* which we watched last night on the video and since it is almost time for the "new season" to start on NBC I must make sure he is Philip so we can make *Miami Vice*. And then he said when you get back home to Nebraska you can tell your friends who complain all the time that there are too many Negroes in the entertainment industry (tho they do not call them Negroes but "porch monkeys" which you and I do not say because it is not refined) that there are not too many Negroes at all. Just the one.

Well Don and Philip left to go back to Miami and Mr. Tom Cruise he said I have some friends coming over tonight the Brat Pack I want you to "be nice" to them Carrie you know what I mean and this time I DID know but I did not think I could be nice to the entire Brat Pack it would be worse than DeWitt's survival team because the Brat Pack are younger men tho cleaner probably.

Well so I called the Jewish man who took me to Las Vegas and said if I ever needed anything to just give a holler and said I want to go home to Nebraska will you help me get there? And Mr. Cohen he said of course I will help you if you will do me one favor and I said of course I will you are so nice you always treated me "like a gentleman." And so he picked me up in a stretch limo at Mr. Tom Cruise's mansion on Rodeo Drive and when I got in he kissed me on the cheek and poured me a glass of Don Paragon. And I did not take nothing from Tom only my clothes.

Well Mr. Cohen he said I want you to deliver a package for me and in exchange for that I will fly you back to Nebraska, and I said I will be glad to if it does not contain nothing illegal and he said of course it does not only a present for a friend. He gave me the package and took me to the airport and I was back in Omaha in no time flat but before I met his friend I went to the ladies room and looked in the package and found that it was full of drugs! The dreaded crack was in there and other things I had never even seen and since I did not want to spend "24 Hours on Crack Street" I flushed all of it down the toilet except the pound of sinsemilla which is another name for real good marijuana which grows wild all over Nebraska you must have seen it yourself and if God put so much of it here it could not be wrong to harvest His bounty even if it is against the law. I put the sinse in my suitcase and took it home and did not wait for Mr. Cohen's "friend."

Well now I am back with DeWitt, it is just like it used to be no worse no better. DeWitt gave me a videotape produced by some of his friends in the Movement called "Woman: What Is Her Position?" starring Mrs. D. Frank Copeland the wife of some big Klan muckety-muck who looks a hundred years old and thinks it is a sin to wear makeup. She quotes the Scripture for a whole damn hour, woman thy name is modesty, she says and blah blah blah. HE TESTS ME ON IT!!! And when DeWitt's brother Ben saw me watching he said Carrie I'll tell you what the position of woman is, the position of woman is prone. Ben laughed and laughed but DeWitt and I did not until Ben explained what "prone" meant and then DeWitt laughed too even if Ben did steal the line from some Negro agitator or so he said later tho he used the other word that you will not print in your magazine because it is not refined and DeWitt didn't like that part much, he stopped laughing. But then he said you gotta hand it to 'em where broads are concerned. They never put down the whip like the White Man did.

The sinse helps the time go by but the phone keeps ringing. Mr. Cohen says he wants to pick up where we left off and that I could make a heap of money in Vegas where there are lots of Fat Admirers who get bored with showgirls all day. I should never of told him my real name. And Roger calls too. He says some bad men are after me but I do not know why. I was never in Humboldt County last summer as you can see from this True Confession. I never stole no dope or agreed to be a mule for Steve who wanted to put me on the street just like Mr.

Cohen does because he was tired of looking at my plug-
ugly corn-fed face glued to the goddam tube all day and
reading them trashy mags at the same goddam time with
my big ass spread across the couch like butter but "In-
quiring minds want to know! *I* want to know!" and since
your so fucking boring Carrie WHY DON'T YOU JUST SPLIT
RIGHT NOW so why is my brother worried? I was in Hollywood the whole time as I have explained in this True
Confession. I haven't seen Steve in years. But Roger says
if Kearney was closer I'd be dead all ready, there are
some people Carrie you just can't fuck with and tho
DeWitt is armed and dangerous they'll get around to me
eventually but when he finds out what I done he will not
protect me, he will call it Adultery, he will cast me out
like Jezebel and the dogs will eat my bones so please
send the money now to Carrie Jo Starkweather. I do not
want to survive, I want to LIVE.

# The Animal in Her

## 1 *the heart of africa*

Nicole: back in the saddle. For five years she'd been *recovering* exploring other options, she was afraid it would fall through but a done deal was a done deal, it was right to go with ICM, they had really come through for her, she was a writer slash director again, but now here she is in Africa which is not where she's supposed to be but she pretends it's all right so as not to alarm the executive producers, circling like jackals, just waiting for her to *flip out* make an error. There are lots of cuddly photogenic animals around and since she's making a movie about animal liberation why is she so nervous? Where's the camera anyway? Did somebody forget the film?

The animals cavort and play *some kind of deer or something* and oh, here's a young one nuzzling her hand, this will make a nice shot *for Walt Disney* so can you get in a little closer honey? she says. Get a nice tight closeup of the wet cold nose nuzzling my hand please, but before she can wonder why she's calling the cameraman honey he's nuzzling her neck and his nose is as cold as the baby deer thing's and her arms go back around him and she forgets about the movie because not only is he her cameraman but her cameraman slash husband Teddy who died five years ago in Nicaragua for her and everybody else *exploded* and she actually heard this at a Sandinista fundraiser, from somebody who didn't know who she was: that it was too bad it wasn't somebody really famous, like Susan Sarandon. And Nicole agreed. But Teddy filmed the whole thing, right up to the last, fucking Susan Sarandon couldn't have done that, and the camera survived though Teddy didn't, the whole thing was on the news for days and days. Aaton even asked about using it in an ad. Nicole shrieked at them for thirty minutes or so, then said yes because Teddy loved his camera. But the ad never came out.

Teddy's mouth feels so good on the back of her neck that she isn't going to think about how her cowboy died with his camera on, she is going to forget about that small fact entirely *dead* until he manages to turn her around and get his hands under her clothes *with pieces of somebody else in the coffin* and make love to her the way only Teddy can, nobody's touched her that way, not for years and years only Teddy, only in her dreams and even there she doesn't get to see him very often, her dreams are as rotten as her afternoons, which she spent watching soap operas before she snapped out of it to do the movie, she was all right so make the most of it, Nicole, she thinks, enjoy, but SOMETHING'S HAPPENING WITH THE ANIMALS.

She brushes Teddy off and tells him to get the camera because a big lion who looks like he hasn't eaten for weeks is sneaking up on the little deer things, but wouldn't you know it, wouldn't you just goddam know it, the magazine's run out and Teddy hasn't got another one ready and of course he hasn't hired a camera assistant anything to save a buck that's my Teddy but you couldn't take it with you after all, could you, honey? It all ended up with me. He's sitting cross-legged on the African veldt with a black changing bag in his lap and a smile on his face, lit cigarette plastered to chapped lower lip, God you look stupid, Teddy, *loading magazines* while the lion stalks the cuddly animals, it's the shot of a lifetime and she is NOT GETTING IT and she isn't gonna put up with this action, no way, Teddy, dead or red, whatever, YOU'RE FIRED!

If she can't get the shot she can at least save the deer things. One of them's run over to where she's standing with the sound man, it's under her hand so she squats down and soothes it. The dry grasses tickle her crotch, her panties are off, her pubic hair is dreadlocked with silver beads, heavy but not unattractive. She gentles the deer thing, tells it to keep its little head down while she takes care of that pesky ole lion with her trusty revolver—only where is it? Does one of the natives have it?

"Give me my gun," she says and the loyal African retainer puts the gun in her hand, but there's no need to use it after all. The deer things have grown impressive horns, they're more like Bullwinkles now, they're tearing the lion apart, there's blood everywhere, it's great but her cameraman slash husband Ted the Dead is still sitting cross-legged on the goddam veldt, changing the goddam magazine. Then the Bullwinkles tear the lion apart completely, only now he looks more like a saber-toothed tiger. As he dies his rib cage flies out of his body, it has little white wings on it, and his heart is inside the rib cage, all festooned with ribbons like a Christmas wreath. It flies straight for Nicole and hovers like a helicopter. Then the wings crumple, the heart stops beating, the whole thing collapses right in front of her, and Nicole knows this is the heart of Africa. But she didn't get the shot.

And at her feet the deer thing isn't an animal anymore but an African woman and she's in labor, she's having a baby right now there's blood everywhere and Nicole calls for Teddy but Teddy doesn't come he's *back in his grave* finally finished loading the magazine and now he's shooting something, a herd of zebras moving across the horizon at sunset, the colors are hot and vibrant, like being on acid. What a great shot, that's so beautiful, Teddy, you're so fucking talented. He's standing there like a tall *dead* tree, the Aaton perched on his shoulder like a cat, my darling, my human tripod, my bear, so tall and steady that when they walked through a Guatemalan market he could hold the camera up high, lock his elbows, and shoot down into the baskets the women carried on their heads, like a crane shot without the crane.

Teddy was her conscience and now that he's gone she doesn't have a conscience, she has ideas, and if I disturb him he might muck up the shot, so she wipes away her tears of joy at being next to the love of her life again, who knows how long it will last, and looks down at the African woman who has the same sad eyes as the baby deer thing, but who is not so photogenic with her teeth like old ivory and neither is the baby coming out of her in slime and blood, is it even breathing? Nicole doesn't touch them. She doesn't want to dirty her hands. Her tears dry up at once. She walks away toward Teddy, the zebras, and the sunset, and is this what they mean when they say WASPs hate people but they love animals?

## 2   *the wolf at the door*

She is Jill Foster Abbott, the villainess slash star of *The Young and the Restless*, sitting in the passenger seat of a speeding car driven by her secretary David who has the hots for her in a big way but Jill won't give him the time of day, he isn't rich or powerful enough. The car whips around curves, tires screeching. Jill doesn't ask David why he's driving so fast. She knows. Something is chasing them.

And in the back seat is Carol, secretary to John Abbott, Jill's former husband and President of Jabot Cosmetics of which Jill owns 20 percent, post-divorce, but it wasn't easy getting it, she used all manner of dirty tricks which Jill isn't above, she clawed her way up from the gutter all right and goddam proud of it too. Carol has a limp and Jill would just as soon fire her but John thinks it's good business, hiring the handicapped and in such a public position too, and Jill thinks he's probably right though she thinks it would be more seemly for Carol to go to a nice home somewhere and not be seen but of course she can't say that out loud. Carol is screaming. No, whining. Typical.

Jill looks out the window and sees that they're being chased by a wolf pack though they don't look like ordinary wolves with their Ray Bans and frayed Armani ties and ears poking through their Stetsons. And Jill thinks maybe she can deal with whiny Carol once and for all and the wolf pack too, kill two birds with one stone so to speak and all without any severance pay or lawsuits from those groups that protect the whining handicapped, it's so fucking brilliant only Jill Abbott could've come up with it, she's proud as she reaches into the back seat and picks up poor long-suffering Carol by the nape of the neck and says, "Carol, this is going to hurt me more than it hurts you," and opens the car door and shoves her out, into the wolf pack.

Jill looks at David and smiles. She takes out a cigarette, puts it in her mouth. David lights it. "This will buy us some time," she says.

David smiles too. "Unfortunately, not enough."

Jill looks back. The wolf pack is gaining again. They finished poor Carol off in no time flat. Jill looks for her silver-plated revolver. Where is it? She remembers giving it to David for some reason. Why in the world would she ever do that? "Give me my gun, David," she says. David opens his coat. The gun is strapped to his left hip. He doesn't give the gun to Jill.

Jill leans back in her seat. She thinks about Jack Abbott, her former stepson. She had an affair with him while she was married to John. That's what caused the divorce. That's why she got all the stock, to keep the scandal out of the papers. She thinks about how long it's been since she's had sex. They wrote her lawyer slash boyfriend out of her life over a year ago. What was his name? She can't remember. He wasn't any good anyway. The last really good sex she had was with Sven, the psychotic masseur, who shot her, then fucked her, then buried her alive. But he did have nice hands. It was scary fucking him, exciting too. But then she was played by another actress.

If she could just materialize Jack Abbott right now she could have some of that before the wolf pack closed in. He liked doing it anywhere, anytime, just like she did. God knows she got little enough now. The goddam writers had done a number on her. They'd turned her, Jill Abbott, into a workaholic who thought about her son all the time, her son, little what's-his-name. She didn't have time for sex now. Her! Jill Abbott! How could they do it? How could she have let them? But there was still time for some fun with Jack, if only she could concentrate. No, focus. Overwrite the writers. But Jack didn't appear.

Oh, well. There was always David, in a pinch. But when Jill opened her eyes to give him that patented Jill Abbott come-hither-and-plug-my-every-orifice smile, David was gone. A giant wasp was driving the car. He had something between his legs all right, but it wasn't exactly what she had in mind, it looked sharp and lethal as it moved in and out, in and out, like a beating heart. The wasp thing grabbed her hair and pushed her head down. It tasted good, actually. Sweet and cold. Blow jobs are always better in dreams. She tried to materialize Jack to deal with the rest of her, but she couldn't concentrate. When the wasp thing came, Jill came too. Her mouth was full of honey when he broke her perfect nose with the gun butt and shoved her out the door, to the wolf pack. Jill never had a chance to make some wisecrack like "Why, David, I didn't know you had it in you." As she fell, she thought of Jack, who had a way with orifices.

## 3 *sheep's clothing*

She had directed a werewolf picture. No, a teenwolf. God help her. Why? She couldn't remember directing it, the picture she'd signed for was about animal liberation, but then again there was her name on the screen. DI-RECTED BY NICOLE WALSH it said, so she must have directed it though she couldn't really tell you when. She said she'd never sell out but she had, obviously. Somebody had finally asked her to. If Teddy were alive, he'd never forgive her. She hopes they paid her a lot of money.

They were watching the picture at Grauman's Chinese Theater. What was happening now? How could it be her picture when she couldn't remember the plot? Her star was in the mountains on some werewolf-killing expedition. He had an anti-werewolf weapon disguised as a ghetto blaster, but when he turned it on, it would kill him too! He didn't know he was a werewolf. Oh, no! "This picture makes absolutely no sense, Nicole," someone whispers. "AND YOU DIRECTED IT!"

Nicole is in the picture then, anything to get out of the audience, and she tries to straighten the plot out by getting the teenwolf away from the weapon and back home, but first they have to stop in a clearing somewhere and have sex, and that's okay too, but quick, he's only sixteen, and Nicole's distracted, she's still trying to direct. Then after the sex scene, the actor playing the teenwolf is replaced by Arnold Schwarzenegger—*impeccable timing, fuckhead*—and they climb to a tall mountain. Nicole holds on to the back of Arnold's belt like she used to hold on to Teddy's when she was tired and climbing the five flights to their apartment and she thinks about Teddy and wonders where he is. Why isn't he at the opening holding her hand and kvetching about Hollywood? Did he shoot this picture for her or not? It doesn't look like his work, that shot's so shaky it's pathetic, he should have used a Steadicam, shouldn't he? But Teddy had never needed one. Jesus. There's even a boom in it. Nicole cries. Teddy would never ruin her movie like this, not unless he stopped loving her.

Then they come upon a herd of sheep, and one of them gets up on her hind legs and walks and Arnold shaves all the wool off her face and she's actually quite attractive in a lime green Stephen Sprouse coat and witty too, she cracks a number of jokes Nicole cannot remember though she wants to write them down in the morning and use them in a screenplay or in her documentary, if she ever gets to make it, which she probably won't since this turkey is going to lay such an egg.

Then she and Arnold go to a party and meet a whole bunch of the sheep slash people, and one of them is Victor Newman, the cruel industrialist from *The Young and the Restless*, and Nicole has the immediate hots for him and tries to flirt by telling him how he should write a book about his days as a sheep called "I Was a Leg of Lamb." Nicole will send it to her agent at ICM, if she still has an agent after this picture opens which she probably won't. Victor Newman is interested in her, sort of.

"And are you married?" he asks with a generic European accent.

"My husband is dead."

"I'm sorry to hear that. Who killed him?"

Nicole wakes up, alone, as always.

"Animals," she says.

# Famous Last Words

Daisy was tipsy when she got out of the car. This was more or less an everyday occurrence. Daisy was often tipsy and often getting out of cars, which her nouveau friends call limos.

It was no use criticizing her. Daisy hated criticism. She didn't know how to take it. "Why should I?" she'd sneer.

"I only had one!" she'd say indignantly, if I complained about her drinking. Only one she'd *paid* for. Some strange new man, some bartender would've bought the rest. Bartenders uptown and down bought her drinks galore. Even the gays poured her triples.

Daisy shared a fond goodbye with the driver, sashayed into the Horseshoe Bar, greeted everyone she knew far too loudly, then plopped down and gave me a wet boozy kiss.

"Your agent called," I said. Those used to be the magic words, but they didn't make her face light up the way they used to. Everyone we knew had trouble reaching their agents, if they *had* agents. They couldn't get their agents to return their calls and were constantly bemoaning this fact. Daisy's agent couldn't get her to return *his* calls. She couldn't be bothered. In addition to her New York literary agent, she had a Hollywood agent now,

17

for her screenplays, as yet unwritten (but they were all sure she could do it).

"How does the number two hundred and fifty sound?" Daisy was saying.

"Two hundred and fifty what?" I said listlessly.

"Two hundred and fifty *what*? Thousand *dollars*. For the movie rights! I've been in meetings all afternoon. Haven't you heard a word I said?" I didn't answer. "Haskell . . . you haven't, have you? You never listen to me anymore."

" 'You never listen to me anymore,' " I mimicked, seizing the moral high ground, though it's true of course. She's right, as usual. My girlfriend Daisy is always right. I hardly ever do listen. "Is it time for our nightly fight? If it is, let's have it now. Let's get it over with. Ding, ding, ding! Round one!"

"I don't *want* to fight, Haskell," said Daisy miserably.

"Oh, I know. You never want to do any of the things you do. But you just can't help yourself."

"Please, let's drop it," she pleaded.

"Okay," I said petulantly, not meaning it.

"Let's *really* drop it, okay? Haskell?" she said in her sexiest voice, the one she uses on the telephone and in the bedroom, the one that always melts me.

"Oh, you mean *really* drop it?" I said. Daisy nodded happily. She knew I was hers, would be hers always, no matter how hard I tried to forsake her. "Really, really, *really* drop it?"

Daisy leaned over and kissed me sweetly. Two or three people applauded. We held the kiss for a long time. After I broke it off, Daisy picked up her drink and toasted the bar.

"This portion of the Haskell and Daisy show, brought to you by Martell, breakfast of champions," she said in a phony voice. I reached over the bar for a napkin and wiped the lipstick off my mouth. Daisy went on with her performance. She loves to be the center of attention.

\* \* \*

Daisy thought I was rich when she met me, because of my name, du Pont. It was an honest mistake. I had all the accoutrements: the loft, the summer home, the education (Yale and, before that, Groton, which Daisy cannot even pronounce). But only my name was rich. What money I'd had was gone. There would be more, of course, somewhere down the line, but there wasn't any just *yet*. I didn't point this out to Daisy until she'd already moved in. By then it was too late. We were in love.

Daisy didn't leave me when I told her I couldn't support her, although she probably should have. She isn't *that* mercenary; people think she is. My friends all think she moved in with me due to my alleged richness, that she needed a man to ride on while she finished the novel about her sordid past. That she would bleed and then discard me like a napkin, stained with her lip prints. This is an image she tries hard to cultivate: the calculating blond bombshell, the material girl. Daisy calls herself "the thinking man's Madonna." She's writing the remake of *How to Marry a Millionaire*. When she has the time—between lunches, meetings, dinners, parties—Daisy works on the treatment.

When Daisy found out about my money, or lack of it, she laughed her big tremendous laugh, never once complained, then took me out for an extremely expensive dinner at Siracusa, our neighborhood bistro. All the dinners, up to then, had been on me. She thinks it's an enormous joke, my being a du Pont and not being rich. But Daisy loves surprises. I actually heard her say this once, on the telephone: "I landed a du Pont all right, but he's the *wrong one*!" When I walked into the room during that conversation, Daisy didn't even look embarrassed. She threw me a kiss. She *waved*. She knew about my job, of course, with the New York Symphony Orchestra, reading unsolicited would-be symphonies. She knew I didn't support myself composing. No one does, almost. But for some reason Daisy thought I worked for *fun*.

After we ate every morsel of the sea creatures, the salads, the pasta, the gelato, washed down by several wines that cost the earth, all paid for by Daisy, who had absolutely no money at all to speak of, my true love took me home and dragged a battered suitcase out from under the bed.

"In this briefcase," she said solemnly, "are ten basic patents." When I failed to laugh as expected, Daisy explained patiently that she was quoting from a movie, *The Man Who Fell to Earth*, one of her favorites. (I saw ten movies a year, tops, before I met Daisy; now I see ten a month.) She was quoting the scene where the spaceman, David Bowie, gives his lawyer, Buck Henry, the key to immense wealth and power.

In Daisy's suitcase were fifteen short stories she wrote in Birmingham, Alabama. She went there to make the transition from coke dealer to literary lion, moving in with a high school boyfriend for the requisite six months. Six *months*. Not because she joined the anti-drug bandwagon, Daisy protests. She finds former druggies who recant in *poor taste*. I laughed at this line when I heard it, coming from Daisy, of all people, but for once I agreed with her. All that breast-beating, that mea culpa, *is* a teeny bit tacky.

"I didn't stop doing coke because it was bad or addictive," Daisy says to one and all, although once, in a weak moment, she admitted she'd done coke "in moderation" every day *for six years*. "I stopped because it was boring," Daisy says.

Jeff, the hometown boyfriend, was a writer too, or used to be. He couldn't write a word while he lived with Daisy.

"I wonder why?" she asked innocently, when she told me this story. It was all I could do to keep from popping her one. Jeff, the poor sucker, finally kicked her out. Daisy thinks he did the right thing.

"He was very honest about it. I respect that. He admitted he couldn't stand the heat," Daisy says generously, although she is not always so fair, so *reasonable*.

She still holds a grudge against a famous lead guitarist who left her under somewhat more acrimonious circumstances, the day he heard her first album, or so she claims. He *said* he was leaving for another reason entirely, for another woman ("A bimbo! In leopard-skin polyester!" says outraged Daisy), that professional jealousy had nothing to do with it. He just didn't love her. But Daisy knows better.

"Why didn't he just *admit* it?" she often agonizes. Not love *Daisy*? This particular relationship stuck in her craw. "Why didn't he just *say* he couldn't stand the heat?"

Daisy hates being left, or rather, being told to leave. She's never had her own apartment. There is no lease anywhere with Daisy's name on it, no insurance policy either. After this Jeff fellow kicked her out, Daisy returned to New York, with the precious suitcase. Two days later, she met me. A week after that, I asked her to move in.

"Publish or perish," Daisy said cheerfully as she showed me the stories. I thought she was joking. I didn't know her yet. The next day, she hustled a free Xerox machine and sent the copies out. I watched her address fifteen envelopes.

"Who do you know at *The New Yorker*?" I asked, peering over her shoulder.

"Nobody," Daisy said.

"Nobody!" I laughed at her. "You don't have a chance! People kill to get into *The New Yorker*."

Daisy turned to me with a big grin on her face that transformed, before my eyes, into a hideous grimace. She got up, stuck one stiff arm out in front of her, and walked toward me, that awful look on her pretty face, dragging one leg: the mummy. Even I know that one. But her voice was pure Lugosi.

"Zo? . . . You zay people . . . *keel*, to get into *Ze New Yorker*?" Daisy took one step forward.

"Stop that!" I said, laughing nervously.

"Famous . . . last . . . *woooords*," Daisy growled, before she attacked.

Daisy was a wonderful actress. Soon, I found out how good a writer she was too. I knew she was pretty and funny and smart and sexy as hell, of course. That was enough. What more do you want in a girlfriend? But I didn't know she was *good*. I didn't *want* to know. I never read any of her work, it never occurred to me to, though she listened to all my tapes right away. Quietly. Re*spect*fully. With a sweet little smile on her face.

"I guess I just don't understand modern art, honey," she said, after the tapes were over, then applied herself to proving how very little it mattered.

By the time the first of the stories was published and the agents started to call, Daisy's gossip-laden *roman à clef* about her first two successful careers, as a seminal— "ovarial," feminist Daisy says—punk rocker (Daisy and the Ch-Ch-Chains) and coke dealer (to the stars!) was almost finished. It took less than a year to write. I know. I watched her. Daisy wrote like the wind in her tiny office. In my big studio, in the front of our Bond Street loft, I didn't write a note, for some strange reason. I hadn't for the whole time we'd lived together.

(Daisy doesn't sing anymore—except to me, alone, in bed—but to keep her hand in, she still penned the occasional rock-and-roll anthem. One of them, based loosely on our relationship, was recorded by her pal Joan Jett and is, even now, on the jukebox at the Horseshoe Bar. When we walk in, people get out their quarters. They play it so often, I don't hear it anymore, though the song, "Free Money (Growin' on Your Family Tree)" has one verse that goes something like this: *Free money/What did you ever see/Free money/In a third-generation white-trash bastard like me?* This was one of the reasons I found it difficult to take Daisy home to Mother. Daisy didn't tell me about "Free Money" until everyone else in town had already heard it. When the moment of truth arrived, Daisy said sweetly, "I hope you're not mad at me.")

After a score of pricey lunches, Daisy settled on a wizened oldster, Wallace Stein, who sold *Unchained*, a.k.a. *Daisy Duke Fulfills Her Early Promise*, for a fat but not inflated fee, which Daisy squandered, once she got her hands on it, more or less immediately. Daisy's gleeful description of their pivotal lunch, at the Russian Tea Room: "Wallace started to light the filter on his cigarette. His flunkies were all afraid to stop him. I plucked it out of his mouth and turned it around. He fell in love with me on the spot!" Wallace Stein gave her an advance against her advance, to pay off her credit cards, buy new clothes, and go to a fat farm in Florida, where she dropped the twenty pounds accrued living with me and wrote an episode of *Miami Vice*, forthcoming. I didn't want her to go. I told her I loved her, just the way she was, although she *had* developed some tiny pimples on her chin from the chocolate I bring her while she's working, the cognacs we share in bed.

"The bigger the cushion, the sweeter the pushin'," I said playfully one night, inside her, trying to talk her out of Florida.

Daisy laughed but didn't eject me. "Is that all I am to you?" she asked. "A *cushion*?"

The second time I tried that line, in more or less the same circumstances and in an admittedly lame parody of the cracker accent she can turn on and off at will, completely forgetting, as I tend to do, that I'd used it once already, Daisy pushed me away and said, "Haskell . . . please. Don't try to be 'down home.' It doesn't become you."

When I persisted in telling her how I didn't want her to go to Florida, Daisy got drunk and screamed the following: "You think if I'm fat, no other man will want me! But I'll tell you a secret, Haskell. I'll *never* get *that* fat!" Right you are, Daisy. Someone will always want you. There will always be a certain kind of man who takes one look at Daisy—fat or thin—and says, grubby hands outstretched like a three-year-old, "That! Gimmie! I want it!'' I never thought I was that kind of man. Now I know that I am.

After Daisy got back from Florida, tan and beautiful, her agent took her to parties. Without me. This hurt somewhat.

''You know you hate parties,'' the new improved Daisy said during this period. She was right again. I loathe parties. I hate meeting new people. We have far too many friends already. I only want Daisy, at home, alone. But that was what made her *fat*, Daisy says. All that home-staying. ''You'd be bored to tears, Haskell.'' Right, right, right, right. Always right. Everything my Daisy says makes sense, but none of it really matters.

We had to walk home from the Horseshoe Bar, although it was below freezing. I'd forgotten to bring money, one of my many grievous faults, a second of which is not having money to *bring*. Daisy paid the whole tab. She barely had enough for the tip. When we left the bar, she was still digging in her purse for change and shooting me these angry, hurt glances.

''What are you thinking about?'' I asked on Fifth Street, as Daisy clomped along martyrlike on red high heels. ''Leaving me?'' Daisy shook her head. A tear trickled down her frozen cheek. ''Are you thinking about leaving me?''

''I love you, Haskell,'' she said sadly, drawing her coat around her tight. She still wore the Burberry I bought her in London, only now it was lined with mink. Under it, Daisy wore ancient Levi's, three-hundred-dollar heels, and a green, gold, and black sweater she found on Charles Street, in the garbage.

''Look, honey! An Issey Miyake!'' Daisy said as I tried to drag her away.

''Put that filthy thing down!'' I ordered, but Daisy ignored me.

''Why would anyone throw out an Issey Miyake?'' she

wondered, brushing coffee grounds off the sweater and cramming it into her purse.

"It's not even your size," I said nastily. "It's much too small." But it wasn't. Daisy repaired a rip in the sleeve and had it cleaned. The sweater fit perfectly. Daisy looked wonderful in it. (One of Daisy's favorite jokes is as follows: Two black garbagemen are driving down the street with a full load and something starts to fall off the truck. One of the men climbs on top of the garbage to hold it on. Two Jewish ladies are walking down the street, the truck goes by, and one of them says to the other, "Look, Ethel! Somebody's thrown out a perfectly good *schwartze*!")

On the Bowery, Daisy started clowning around. She walked on the curb, her hands straight out, and let one shoe drag in the muck like a peglegged pirate. *Up* and down, *up* and down. Then she burst into song: *"One foot in the door. The other one in the gutter."* Daisy glanced at me, waiting for the laugh. I ignored her.

"I know you love me, but that won't stop you from leaving, will it?" I said peevishly. Daisy straightened up. "It won't stop you when someone *really* rich comes along. Some rock star. Some movie producer."

"I've *had* rock stars," Daisy said. "I've *had* movie producers."

"By the thousands, no doubt," I said sarcastically. I have no idea how many boyfriends Daisy has actually had. During the Gary Hart debacle, she joked that if she ever went into politics, she'd type up a list of them and hand it out. It would take about five pages, she said.

"Single-spaced or double-spaced?" I asked sarcastically. Daisy actually had to think about this one! Up to that point, when I saw her mulling the question over in her mind, right in front of me, not even bothering to hide her thought processes, I assumed she was being facetious. When she noticed my ashen face, she pretended it was all a joke. But it wasn't. "I was sort of wild, honey, before I met *you*," Daisy said.

"What I want now is you, Haskell," Daisy went on resolutely. "If you don't want me to leave, you know what you can do about it."

Marry her, she meant. Marry her or lose her.

"Let's not talk about that," I said lamely.

"Fine, let's not talk about it. But time's getting short." She'd given me a deadline. A *deadline*! I couldn't believe it. I thought she was joking. I hoped she was. "At least *think* about it, Haskell."

I thought about it all the time. I loved her, but I didn't want to marry her. *Couldn't*. There wasn't money now, but there would be. But not if I married Daisy. Mother had made that quite clear. Taking Daisy to meet her was the worst mistake, absolutely and relatively, I'd ever made in my life. It had been a nightmare, a disaster. I had no idea anything could possibly be so *bad*.

"She'll love you, darling," I told the recalcitrant Daisy, who had been to Fishers Island before, with someone else, and had an awful if memorable time. "She'll love you. She'll *have* to. Exactly the way I do," I said. But she didn't. Daisy often had this effect on women. At the MacDowell Colony, a distinguished painter took a dislike to Daisy on sight. Behind Daisy's back, she called Daisy "Scarlett." When Daisy heard about this, she loved it. She *roared*. Soon everyone was calling Daisy "Scarlett." By going public with the insult, Daisy defused it. She *thanked* the painter for the lovely new nickname. What the painter replied, sweet Daisy never said.

Taking Daisy to Fishers was like flinging popcorn on a hot stove. She alienated Mother completely in each and every way, arriving at the Big Club for the Thursday night buffet in a black spandex mini and six-inch platform sandals—"Where'd you get those shoes, Daisy? Times Square?" my cousin Walter said, efficiently setting the stage for what was to follow—her white-blond hair Tenaxed two feet straight up, in full makeup, then guzzling far too many bullshots and captivating, *kissing*, some decrepit billionaire who Mother, as a young widow, had once had a fling with and, judging by her response to Daisy, still coveted. (Daisy flirts with most men and some women. I've long since stopped chastising her for it.) Then Daisy compounded her already grievous errors by telling Mother, bastion of the Protestant work ethic, that rich people and poor people always get along better with each other than either group does with the middle class, because they're both lazy and enjoy their sloth. Only the middle class feels compelled to work. That certainly did tear it, all right. When Mr. Forsythe, the billionaire, trained his rheumy old eyes on her cleavage once too often, Daisy rapped his naked pate twice with a bejeweled knuckle. "Anybody home?" she said.

My Daisy ate like a bird—a *vulture*. She particularly like the billibi. "Ooooooh! Are those matzo balls?" she had shrieked to all and sundry while dishing out the cold mussel soup. On her third trip to the soup tureen, Daisy lost an earring. Two hours later, Bunky Arrington almost choked on it.

The next night, at Grey Gulls—where Daisy might have been staying had she landed the right du Pont—my girlfriend, chastened by her hangover, was somewhat more demure, on her best behavior in fact. "Yum-yum! Everything is so *good*," she kept saying enthusiastically, as if Daisy, who is on a first-name basis with every maître d' in every good restaurant in New York, who whines if we spend less than a hundred dollars for a supper, had never had a decent meal in her life.

Need I mention that when Mother asked Daisy what her novel was about, Daisy said honestly, "Drugs, sex, and rock and roll. It's about the gutter, where Haskell found me." And, turning to me: "How does it go, honey? Barefoot and pregnant and chained to some . . . *refrigerator*, or something?"

*Oh, Daisy.* She then proceeded to ignore me for the entire weekend, a fact that did not go unremarked by Mother.

"You treat me just like a stranger," I whined to Daisy, when I got her alone.

"No," she said truthfully. "If you were a stranger, I'd treat you better."

I know Daisy behaves this way because she's insecure, that inside the sophisticate, the femme fatale, the genius, there's a sharecropper's granddaughter spawned by a traveling salesman yearning to get out, or yearning *not* to. If I married her, Daisy says, she'd be far more secure, behave better, and I believe her, somewhat.

Daisy's sojourn on Fishers—chronicled accurately but in a somewhat self-serving manner in Duke, Daisy, "Money Can't Buy You Brains," *The New Yorker*, May 15, 1987, pp. 33–37—reminded many who witnessed it of the brief but unforgettable visit of another New York demi-star, Edie Sedgwick, who arrived for a date with somebody on the prow of Jock Whitney's yacht, like a figurehead. I was there for Edie's debut. I was twelve years old. I had never seen anyone remotely resembling her, glimpsed anything so exotic. In her silver lamé mini-dress, Edie Sedgwick turned cartwheels on the Buckners' lawn. Could this be the key to my infatuation with Daisy, that early glimpse of Edie Sedgwick? Perhaps she was *imprinted* on me, not her physical type of course, for Edie was frail and waiflike where Daisy is robust, voluptuous, but her recklessness, her heedlessness, her talent for making scenes. Is this why I gave my heart to Daisy, why my reckless, heedless heart rushed headlong toward her like a rogue locomotive barreling down the tracks?

Most people, and I am not ashamed to be one of them, avoid conflict, but Daisy conjured conflicts so she could walk over them in her four-inch heels: so she wouldn't be bored. She used the conflicts she created for material. (I always assumed, after we had a fight, that Daisy wrote down everything I said in the notebook she keeps by the bed, in plain sight, never even bothering to hide it, like she fails to hide all her inappropriate, hurtful feelings.

That she used me for material too. But I have never found my name, or words, in her notebooks, though there is a character in them who appears more and more frequently, code name The Hun, with whom Daisy has long, suspiciously witty—imaginary?—conversations.)

Daisy has always lived on the edge, has no idea one can live anywhere else, no concept of what normal life might be. Her favorite movie is *Rebel Without a Cause*. Her favorite director is Russ Meyer. Her favorite singer is Patti Smith. Her favorite song is "Rock and Roll Nigger."

One day, when Daisy was playing "Rock and Roll Nigger" far too loudly through my sensitive speakers, I ventured this comment: "Do you really think the Garrisons *enjoy* listening to this . . . *song*, Daisy, in the dead of night?" The Garrisons are the perfectly respectable black couple who share our floor, have shared it, with me, for the past ten years, although we have never been properly introduced. "Don't you think it might *offend* the Garrisons to hear that blasting?"

"I don't know," Daisy said. "I never actually thought about it."

"Hmph!" I said triumphantly, ridiculously pleased with myself. I almost never win an argument with Daisy. Then Daisy got up off the floor, went next door, *and asked them.* Down the hall, as if from the end of a long, long tunnel, I heard hysterical laughter in three different keys. The next thing I knew, she'd invited them over for drinks. Black people certainly do drink a lot of cognac, I soon ascertained. Almost as much as Daisy. Vicky Garrison had been raised in New Haven, right down the street from campus, and was, I learned within minutes, the daughter of the venerable Professor Alfred Lord Beauregard who had given me a gentleman's C in American History. Vicky, an investment banker at First Boston, who is quite like Daisy, only in blackface, said she didn't mind listening to "Rock and Roll Nigger," "Wake Up Niggers," or "I Wanna Be Black" as long as Daisy and

I could tolerate the odd white-bashing Rasta. John Garrison—who, I found out later, pulls in yearly, without leaving his home, five times my entire net worth—said none of it mattered one way or the other. He has these state-of-the-art earplugs he swears by. Like me, he hates rock and roll.

Daisy always pushes everything far too far. She tests every chain to find its weakest link. Before Daisy settled down with me, men were always putting their fists through walls because of her, their hands or heads through phone booths. They were always getting beaten up by bouncers and sailors, putting cigarettes out on skin. They were always getting drunk and wrecking their cars. ("Why, when David and I were breaking up, we went through three cars in three weeks!" Daisy once said merrily.) They were always calling her from emergency rooms, broken, burnt, or bleeding, and asking her to fill out their insurance forms. (Some of them *still* call, from ten years back, to tell her they love her, to wish her a happy birthday.) Daisy claims she has no idea why they act that way, although she did say once, in a rare candid moment, "They hurt *themselves* to keep from hurting *me*." Daisy swears she never provoked them, but I know better. I know, because since our marriage discussions began, this confrontational behavior of hers has escalated and has been directed, more and more often, toward *me*.

Daisy does the same kind of thing in her work, too, taunting, confronting, taking a perfectly normal situation or character and pushing, *pushing*. . . . Even her unspeakable family finds that a bit much. She airs far too much dirty linen, even for them! When she had skewered one of her relatives, the infamous Uncle Bob, by making him the main character in her witty little send-up of Stephen King, *The Ghoul Next Door* (a.k.a. *Calling All Ghouls, Boys and Ghouls Together, Boy Meets Ghoul, There's a Ghoul in My Soup*, and—my personal favorite—*Ghouls of the Southeast Conference*) her cousin Carlene Diffendaffer—where do they get these *names*, down south?—had called to read her the riot act.

"You've turned Daddy into a MONSTER!" Cousin Carlene reportedly shrieked.

"If the shoe fits . . ." Daisy said provocatively.

(Daisy had dropped Diffendaffer during her rock-and-roll days, in favor of the infinitely more euphonious—not to say shorter—Duke, by which she is now known. But now that Daisy was a serious novelist, she agonized, night after endless night, about reclaiming the mighty name of Daisy Mae Diffendaffer, her heritage, her *roots*. Oh, my. This was the one issue on which her agents, Greenstein and Berg, and I fervently agreed. We all dissuaded Daisy at length from this rash, potentially ruinous, move. It was a fine name, of *course* it was, but the world wasn't ready for Diffendaffer, we argued. Daisy Mae, our little Dogpatch denizen, had relented, finally. We *thought* she had.)

"Maybe by the time the book comes out, it won't matter," Daisy said, directing a pointed glance my way. Daisy Duke, née Diffendaffer, wanted to be a du Pont before her novel went to press. (The name alone, she said, would sell an extra ten thousand copies.) She wanted to be married. To me, or somebody else. Preferably to me. She *loves* me.

"I'm too old for all this . . . *indecision*," Daisy says often. She has just turned thirty.

"I never thought I'd make it!" she said gaily, during her birthday party, thrown for her at Le Cirque by Steinberg and Green. (One may have noticed I can never tell them apart. Daisy calls me an anti-Semite for it.) "I never thought I'd live this long," Daisy said. "Now I want to live *forever*!"

After her novel came out, I wouldn't be *able* to marry Daisy. I wouldn't be able to afford to. She actually *said* this: "If you wait till the book comes out, I'll be too famous to marry you." She said it *cheerfully*, with a tender kiss. Maybe Daisy was joking, but somehow I didn't think so. If I didn't marry her, I'd lose her. If I married her, I'd lose the money, and I *still* might lose her. "Forever" wasn't in Daisy's vocabulary. Even if I married her, she'd leave me one day, for somebody richer, more famous, more attractive, some over-the-hill rocker, director, or poet (Daisy went for those grizzled burnout cases), some Nobel Prize winner, congressman, or high school senior. ("You know what they say about sex with young boys?" Daisy actually said once. "It's like cafeteria food. It's bad, but there's so much *of* it." Daisy laughed merrily, then noticed me, as usual, far too late. "Of course, I wouldn't know personally," guilty Daisy said then, attempting a straight face.) She'd leave me for some genius, certified by the MacArthur Foundation, some carpenter who put his cigarettes out in beer cans. She'd leave me and say sincerely, really believing it, as she was walking out the door with her suitcase—filled to the brim with another new career—that she was doing it for *me*, for my own good.

By the time we got home, Daisy was shivering and sniffling, wiping snot off her nose with the back of her hand and onto her jeans, a gesture she knows I hate. Daisy never carries handkerchiefs, or even Kleenex. Her sicknesses come on dramatically, like everything else. I knew she would toss and turn all night, kick off blankets, open windows and close them tight. I wouldn't get a wink of sleep. And the next day she would be sick. She would cancel her appointments and spend the day in bed, reading magazines, making notes for new novels and films and songs and short stories, and talking on the phone to her famous friends, 90 percent of whom are men. And it would all be my fault, of course, for not having cab fare. I'd want to rip the phone out of the wall, but I wouldn't be able to.

Daisy took off her coat and threw it on a chair, then sat down on the couch and thumbed through the *Village Voice* impatiently. I went into the kitchen, took two snifters out of the dish drainer, and examined them critically.

Daisy had washed the dishes that morning, as is her wont every two or three months. She eschews soap and hot water, claiming they're bad for her hands.

"These glasses are disgusting, Daisy," I complained, as I rewashed them. Daisy ignored me. "They still have *lipstick* on them," I persisted. No response. I dried the glasses and poured each of us a cognac.

"There's two thousand maniacs at the Thalia SoHo," Daisy said, as I handed her her drink. Even coming from Daisy, this was too much to bear.

"Are," I corrected. Daisy looked at me blankly. She didn't *write* like a cracker. Why did she have to talk like one? "There *are* two thousand maniacs at the Thalia SoHo," I said firmly. Daisy giggled. I sat down next to her on the couch.

It wasn't until Daisy crawled into my lap and kissed me and said, "You're so funny sometimes. Not *all* the time. But sometimes," that I realized *2,000 Maniacs* was the name of some awful film or band. Daisy thought I'd been making a joke, not an everyday occurrence chez du Pont. I didn't bother to enlighten her.

"Some kind of labor dispute?" I said, with what I perceived to be bone-dry wit. Daisy smiled sweetly, but it was clear that the joke I'd made on purpose hadn't gone over as well as the one I'd made by accident, the one that was really on me, had Daisy but known it. My darling straightened up, took a dainty gulp of cognac, put down the *Voice*, and started going through her mail. I had disposed of most of the postcards, inviting her to this event or that. I always tried to get to the mail first. I discard as much as I can get away with. Daisy caught me at this activity once, but it didn't bother her as much as it might've, though she did begin to make a point, after that, when she could spare the time from her busy schedule, of being around when the mail came.

Somehow, although I got to the mail first that day, I managed to miss a letter from one of the artists' colonies Daisy had applied to for the upcoming summer. She zeroed in on the letter right away and ripped it open impatiently. A big smile lit up her face.

"Honey! I got into MacDowell!" she said. Of course she did. I stood, plucked Daisy's coat from the floor where it had fallen, and went to the closet to hang it up.

"Are you going?" I asked from the bedroom, dreading the answer. She had gone to the MacDowell Colony once before, the previous summer, and had or had not—depending on whether or not she was lying—gotten involved with the immensely rich and famous minimalist composer, Vernon West, whom I loathed, personally and professionally. I tend to think the operative word is "had," though Daisy said not, without denying for a minute that she *could've*, had she but said the magic word, and no one I knew could confirm or dispel the rumor, though I did notice Vernon West's friends looking at me strangely, whenever I managed to drag Daisy, kicking and screaming, to a concert. Daisy said I was just being paranoid, even as she refused to reassure me that she wasn't seeing Vernon West in New York, behind my back. She stood on her constitutional right to silence, since we weren't married.

"You have no need to know," Daisy said solemnly. I screamed, which I do not know how to do effectively. I threw dishes, also an unfamiliar activity. I wept. I piled her meager possessions in the hall. (Later, before dawn, I brought them back inside, before the Garrisons woke up to see.) Daisy wouldn't budge. She wouldn't say a word. Nothing. Not a peep. Just smiled enigmatically, which drives me mad. My jealousy was so consuming, I almost kicked her out. I *tried* to. I couldn't do it. I was too afraid of where she might go: straight to Vernon West?

Once Daisy wrote a song for me, to make up for the lingering scandal of "Free Money." She wrote it in my voice, not hers. It was recorded by the Mekons, none of whom Daisy has slept with, or so she claims. It has a county-and-western tang. It goes like this: *My life began the night we met.* . . . It was right on the money too. I couldn't remember a thing about me, before Daisy. It wasn't even a blur, my alleged life. It just wasn't there.

I don't know whether or not she had, or is having, an affair with Vernon West. I never know whether she's lying or not. I once read a description of Ronald Reagan that fits my darling perfectly: Truth, for Daisy, is what she happens to be saying at the time. But when Daisy got home from MacDowell and we discussed my work—not new work, which I hadn't any of, but old work that I passed off as new (Daisy couldn't tell the difference), not wanting to be just another of Daisy's boyfriends, another ninety-eight-pound weakling who, because of her, couldn't work—she used somebody else's voice to criticize it. Somebody else's words tumbled from her lip-sticked mouth.

"Isn't it just a little bit . . . rigid?" Daisy said tentatively. Daisy knows as much about twelve tone as I know about her favorite band, the execrable Butthole Surfers. I tried to explain the beauty of duodecaphony to her. I put it in very simple terms indeed. But Daisy's green eyes were soon far, far away. Suddenly they focused on a pile of week-old newspapers.

"Honey! Rita Hayworth died!" Daisy said suddenly, with real concern in her voice, cutting me off just like that. She picked up the newspaper and turned straight to the obituaries.

"What a love story!" some drunken friend once gushed. "You're like a . . . a cultural Romeo and Juliet!" Nobody knew what we were doing together, but then again there we were.

"I don't know if I'm going to MacDowell or not," Daisy was saying. "If the movie deal comes through, I won't have to. We'll have our own artists' colony, honey. It's called a summer house."

"You know I can't take the summer off," I said. *But Vernon West could.* Both he and Daisy were ludicrously overpaid for their intermittent labors. Everyone in the entertainment industry was grossly overpaid. I found this revolting. Daisy's income was irregular, but when the checks came in, as they always did eventually, the figures were so large I literally gasped. Daisy cashed the checks nonchalantly and spent the money as fast as she could. She never saved a penny, owned nothing except the clothes on her back, her books, her jewelry, records. When there was no money, she used her charge cards. When the cards were recalled, she obtained more. I had no idea how she did it. She paid taxes something like every five years. When Daisy moved, she left everything behind. I assumed Vernon West did the same.

When I would try to explain the situation to Daisy, which I called the three M's—Mother, Marriage, and Money—in a lame attempt to defuse it, like Daisy herself defused the serious with a joke, she would brush me off. "Make your own money," she'd say impatiently. "*I* did." *So did Vernon West*, she probably thought, but mercifully didn't say. Daisy didn't understand minimalism, but she understood an SRO sign on the box office at Alice Tully Hall, the going rate for an ad endorsing Amaretto or Rose's Lime Juice, the remuneration obtained from being profiled by Dewar's Scotch.

Apropos our summer house, Daisy said this: "You'll come on weekends, like a good little upper-class Daddy. You know the drill."

"Oh, sure. Leave you at the beach all week—"

"Maybe not the beach. Maybe the mountains!"

"Leave you alone with five thousand men! No way!" Daisy smiled with tantalizing obscurity. Only once had I stopped Daisy from doing something she'd wanted to do. When she was beginning the second draft of *Unchained*—armed with ominous briefs from two different law firms and a dog-eared copy of *How to Avoid Libel and Invasion of Privacy Suits*—Todd Rundgren, yet

another old boyfriend, had offered the use of his estate
in Woodstock, to find out if he was in her book, no
doubt.

I wouldn't let her go.

"Daisy . . . I'm putting my foot down," I said.

"You're cute when you're angry, honey." She called
everyone honey: Stein, Greenberg, Todd Rundgren, me,
the plumber, Vernon West.

"I'm not cute at all," I said crossly. I am blond and
fair and average-looking. If the truth be known, I look
like a Republican, a banker, which I would've been
had Schoenberg failed to intervene. ("Men don't get
faces until they're at least forty, honey," Daisy said
once, thoughtfully, studying my pink-and-white bland-
ness. "Women get them much earlier. When you're
forty, you'll have some face!" Like Vernon West, I
thought grimly, as the rugged no-talent smirked at me
from some magazine or other. Vernon West had sold
out, if you could call it that, given where he started, in
a very big way indeed. "I usually don't go for men
who are so . . . all-*American*," Daisy said on our first
date, as she took off my well-fogged glasses. In fact,
Daisy went for any kind of men at all. Her tastes were
catholic in the extreme.)

"Stop saying that!" Daisy said, to my disavowal of
cuteness. "Of course you're cute! All my boyfriends are
cute. It's part of the job description."

Daisy doesn't mind my jealousy. Men are *supposed* to
be jealous. Like cute, it is part of the job description.
Daisy thinks my jealousy means I love her. I guess it
means that, all right, but it also means something else
entirely. (Once Daisy took me to a movie in which Dennis Hopper, a one-legged biker, kills his girlfriend out
of jealousy. Another character, a hulking teenage moron,
kills his girlfriend too. When the two of them discuss the
fine art or science of girlfriend murder, Dennis Hopper,
Daisy's favorite actor but not, officially, an old boyfriend, says this: "But did you *love* her, man? Did you

really *love* her?'' As if *loving* them, really *loving* them, loving them to pieces, as it were, justifies any atrocity. Perhaps it does at that.) Anyway, Daisy didn't go to Todd Rundgren's. She went to MacDowell, where she met Vernon West.

''You know what you can do about it, Haskell,'' Daisy was saying. I didn't say anything back. Of course I knew. ''You know how men make sure their girlfriends are faithful,'' Daisy went on rhetorically.

''Yeah, yeah,'' I said, trying to brush her off.

''They marry them,'' she said. ''Tick, tick, tick.''

In the bathroom, I got down on my knees and banged my head against the tub experimentally, until Daisy came, knocking on the door, asking what the hell I was doing and whether I was all right. I told her I was. The pain made me dizzy for five or ten minutes. It distracted me temporarily from the bigger pain, the one in my heart. But it didn't solve anything. I couldn't marry Daisy. One sees my dilemma. Neither could I live without her.

We got into bed. Daisy had opened the window, as usual, and piled on far too many covers. She turned her back to me and settled into my arms, then nudged me inquisitively with her perfect ass.

While Daisy was bending over the trunk of the car she had rented in order to drive to MacDowell, to Vernon West, stuffing it full of flimsy, inappropriate clothes, our neighborhood crack lord came up to me and said, *mano a mano*, ''You some lucky sumbitch! Man! What a bootie!'' Daisy heard him. She was flattered. She *laughed*. Daisy had an ass like Monroe on the calendar, but when she pressed it against me there was nothing for her, as there had been nothing for me at the piano, and had been nothing for a long, long time. Daisy was being sweet about it, so far. She wouldn't be sweet forever.

Three weeks ago, Daisy lunched with Mother, who is in town, she claims, for the duration, whatever that means. They ate at Mortimer's. I never found out who initiated the lunch, but Daisy came home happy, pleased with herself, *purring*. On the telephone, Mother sounded the same.

The next day, the two of them went shopping. Daisy came home with some sacks from Bergdorf's, full of things Mother had decided to throw out, and a new suit from Adolfo, tomato red. Daisy tried it on for me.

"It *might* look good . . . on Nancy *Reagan*," I said. Daisy swatted me playfully. If Nancy were a size 12, I thought but didn't say. Daisy's putting on weight again, although I haven't pointed it out to her yet, given that of which I live in fear: another trip to the fat farm. Mother's Dior gowns, from the fifties, looked good on Daisy, but Mother never was what you'd call small.

Later that afternoon, I went downstairs to get the mail. There was a letter from Mother in the box, stamped but not canceled. In the letter, Mother withdrew her objections to our marriage, completely and without explanation. I wondered what Daisy did or said to change Mother's mind. Flash her burgeoning bankbook at her?

Upstairs, I positioned the letter prominently, but Daisy didn't mention it. She didn't nag, uncharacteristically. She waited for me to bring it up. When I didn't, she told me the news of the day: Melanie Griffith is going to play her in the film version of *Unchained*; Madonna liked the book, her people said, but it isn't the kind of image she wants to project, for kids. Daisy cursed Madonna colorfully, kissed me, and flew away to an appointment in her new red suit.

When Daisy came home, her hair was a different color and style, kind of blondish-brown, gently curled, almost . . . *natural*. She went to Crown before she came home, she said. Her publicist screamed and screamed, because her new look doesn't match her jacket photo, until Daisy showed him a box with a wig in it, the same color as Daisy's late hair. "Maybe we'll put the wig on tour," the publicist had joked, "and leave you at home." I told Daisy that sounded fine.

"What happened to my little blond bombshell?" I whined.

Daisy laughed. "I'm still your little blond bomb-shell," she said. "In camouflage. For your eyes only." Daisy patted my hand reassuringly. "Don't give up the ship, little buddy."

I poured us a cognac, but Daisy didn't touch hers. She didn't *mention* not touching it either, which is odd. When Daisy goes on the wagon for one or two days, it usually causes quite a stir. She does it with aplomb, with threats to fix me, should I tempt her to fall off. But not now. She's stopped drinking completely, at least around me, and all without saying a word.

As I pondered this new imponderable, Daisy said, out of the blue, "Haskell, I've been thinking. . . . Maybe you should join the Yale Club."

"Where did *that* come from?"

"They have a good health club," Daisy went on, pat-ting my tummy meaningfully. "You know how you hate my friends. We could meet some new people."

"Those aren't new people, darling. They're *old* peo-ple," I said.

"Not to *me*."

I turned on the wide-screen television Daisy forced me to buy when she moved in and pretended to be absorbed in a *Wiseguy* rerun. Daisy dropped the subject, very un-like her, dammit. She was up to something. While I downed my usual cognac, she sipped hot milk, laced with nutmeg and honey. Then she set down her drink and put her head in my lap, didn't even try to change the channel. What's going *on*? I wanted to shriek.

But since Daisy was being so sweet, I decided to hu-mor her, introduce her to some "new" people. She would tire of them soon enough, as I had. I called a number of old friends, who were surprised to hear from me but not displeased, or so it seemed, and a few days later, some invitations did come in. One, for a dinner party at the odious Trump Tower given by some hideous *arrivistes* Mother knew for some reason or other, was seized by Daisy immediately, like the brass ring on the carousel, before I had a chance to throw it out. Daisy jumped up and down until I accepted the invitation, then shopped for a solid week. I hardly saw her at all.

Tonight, before the party, we went to Mother's new digs, for cocktails.

"That dress needs something," Mother had said, looking at Daisy's neckline critically. We all knew what it needed. It needed jewels. Daisy hung her head in shame. Mother eyed me accusingly, as if it were my fault for not providing them. I shrugged, looked heavenward for succor. Mother took Daisy by the hand and led her into the bedroom, settled her at the dressing table, then got her jewels out of the library safe. When Mother opened the jewel case, I saw this look on Daisy's face for the first time: pure *awe*, like a child in a Steven Spielberg film who's just dug up pirate treasure. Mother clasped a number of strands around Daisy's pretty neck, then picked out something simple, in emeralds, which matched Daisy's green eyes, and selected, from her closet, something in sable, which set off my darling's new hair.

"Ooooh, it's just like *The Bonfire of the Vanities*," Daisy whispered to me later in the evening, of the ostentatious Trump Tower apartment, when we were still close, allied. Daisy looked beautiful, but too like the other women there for my taste. I am used to her standing out more, being different. I am used to being the adoring consort, the straight man, while Daisy, the cynosure, bubbles and shines. But this time, among my people, such as they are—the pallid old-monied, like ghosts among the bright young comers—Daisy was sober, reserved, intelligent. Daisy merely fit in, but perfectly. She fit in better than I did. She shone, but gently. No one wanted to talk to me at all. Everyone wanted to talk to Daisy.

Daisy's treatment of me, too, was exemplary. She flirted, but with restraint. She was witty, but never loud. She kept flitting back to me all night, taking my arm, kissing me, claiming me.

Once, I found myself in a corner, talking to Ethel Maytag, with whom I grew up on Fishers. Of dear, square Ethel, this can be said: She excelled at field hockey. Then something strange happened. Ethel's escort came round to claim her, as Daisy was always claiming me, and he was Vernon West! Ethel positively beamed as she introduced us. Vernon West kissed her overtanned cheek.

"It hasn't been announced, but we're engaged, you know," Ethel whispered, after Vernon West departed, Yamamoto dinner jacket in tow, obviously bored with the company.

"Congratulations."

"You congratulate the *man*, Hasky."

"What do you say to the girl?"

"You wish her good luck!"

"Good luck, Ethel," I said, meaning it. *You'll need it.*

"Mummy's not pleased. He's a . . . well, you know." I did, I did. Daisy had told me, in a weak moment, that he had changed his name from Weissberg.

"That explains it," I had said to Daisy, without censoring myself as I usually do, thinking of his so-called music, but how it had sounded was exactly what I meant.

"Explains what?" Daisy asked suspiciously. It was my turn to smile enigmatically. True, there was no place left in New York City where a billion dollars wouldn't buy one in, but Vernon West would never join the Fishers Island Club, no matter how much filthy lucre he amassed.

But neither Ethel nor I said the J word. It just wasn't done, not even in private, not even among old friends.

"Dear Ethel," I said. "Always calling spade a Negro." Ethel tittered and shushed me, though it had been she who, during dessert, had responded to a story about pack llamas in Yosemite with this comment: "But why don't they just use *black* people?"

"I do love him, Hasky," Ethel went on. "He's so . . . well, *fabulous*. I think Mummy's very old-fashioned. Anyway, there's nothing she can do. Not now." Ethel had her own money; there were no trustees to deal with. "I would think you, of all people . . ."

Ethel trailed off, her eyes flickering toward Daisy, who was standing far too close to Vernon West. In front of a Van Gogh, they eyed each other over champagne flutes which, in Daisy's case, held sparkling water.

"Quite," I said. While Ethel babbled on about her wedding plans, I imagined a plot concerning us, something twisty, out of Hitchcock, hatched in a cabin in New Hampshire, over cognacs and drugs and dirty, uninhibited, lower-class sex, the kind Daisy and I never had. It was early spring when they met at MacDowell, cold enough for a fire. And Daisy looked beautiful in firelight. Vernon would marry Ethel and take all her money. Daisy would marry me and take the only thing I had to give: my name. Then they would leave us and marry each other, and travel the world, and create, and have fun. How they would *laugh*.

"Hasky?" Ethel was saying. "You haven't changed a bit, have you, darling? You haven't heard a word I said."

We took a taxi home. Daisy demanded a limousine, but I put my foot down.

"Did you have a good time?" Daisy said, drawing the sable around herself tight, snuggling up. "*I* did."

"Art like that shouldn't be in private homes," I complained.

"Why not?"

"It's obscene. Great art belongs to the public. It should be in museums, where people can see it."

"My, my," Daisy said. "Such a democrat."

"That's what Father did, with *our* art."

Daisy sat up straight. "What?"

"He donated it. I'll take you to visit it sometime."

"He had no right to do that, Haskell—"

"He had *every* right."

"—to deprive you of your inheritance!"

"Daisy! Please! I *agree* with Father. I would have done the same, had it come to me."

"Oh, no, you wouldn't," Daisy said.

"What's that?"

"I wouldn't've let you, honey. I'd kind of like having it around the house, just for us two. What did you think of that apartment?" Daisy went on. "I wouldn't mind living like that, just for a change. Would you?"

"Darling, I *loathe* places like that."

Daisy laughed. "Well, *I* don't."

"Daisy. Darling. Let me tell you something. Let me fill you in on the facts of life. That wasn't just a millionaire's apartment. That was a *billionaire's* apartment. There's a difference, believe me. We'll *never* live like that."

"Oh, I don't know. . . ."

"Never. Not ever. No matter how successful your book is. Not even Stephen King can afford those paintings. Maybe he can afford *one*, but not two dozen. Don't even think about it."

"Then maybe *you* should think about getting a job too."

"*What?*"

"You heard me. A job. J-O-B. A *real* job."

"Daisy! Why are you *talking* like this?"

"At which real money is earned."

"What about my music?"

"Well, you've given it your best shot, after all.

Maybe you're just not cut out for music." Like *you* are. "Maybe it's time to move on. Why don't you talk to your uncle?"

"Earth to Daisy!" I said.

Daisy laughed. Once again, she had gone too far, and she knew it.

"Darling, if I wanted to live in Trump Tower, I would have married Ethel Maytag."

"I didn't know you knew her," Daisy said lightly.

"Certainly I know her. I used to tread on her pudgy toes in dancing school."

"What's she like?" Daisy asked, and this in itself was suspicious. Daisy isn't interested in women.

"Oh, like me," I said.

Daisy smiled. "Seriously."

"Seriously," I said.

"Is she terribly rich?"

"Terribly. But not as rich as she once was. She put a lot of her money into political documentaries in the seventies."

"How impractical of her."

"How indeed."

"She'll be richer one day."

"Oh, yes," I said. "Of course. Richer and richer and richer."

Daisy smiled and drifted away. She was humming the overture, if you could call it that, from one of Vernon West's symphonics.

Daisy didn't know what to do with Mother's emeralds. She paced around the loft trying to think of a place to hide them, then stashed them under a loose board beneath the piano, where she used to keep her cocaine. The sable, though, she threw on the bed. Then she stripped to a black bustier, stockings, and high heels and lay down on the fur. She posed provocatively, a big smile on her face. But when I sat down next to her, reached for her, Daisy slapped my hand away. She didn't want me like that, not anymore. My not wanting *her* like that had gotten to her, finally. Daisy got up, shed her finery in a trice, and slipped on an ancient Alabama practice jersey, number 15. She won't tell me who it once belonged to.

Daisy made me get off the sable so she could hang it up.

"Anyone could come in here and just take it," Daisy agonized, as she checked the locks on the windows and doors for the fiftieth or so time. I sat down on the couch with a drink.

"This building is perfectly secure," I said.

"Even if we had the money, we could never have anything nice."

"Stop it."

"Well, I'm sick of it! I think we should move uptown!"

"But, Daisy," I said, genuinely shocked. "I like it down here in boho land."

"Well, I don't. It's so inconvenient."

"Incon*venient*?" Daisy's *life* was downtown: all her friends, her favorite haunts, her *material*. "And where would my lady *like* to live?"

Daisy swallowed. "Seventy-fifth and Park?"

"Seventy-fifth and *Park*?" I started laughing. "You're dreaming. We can't afford it."

"We could if we sold the loft."

"Not even then."

"Your mother could loan us the money."

"You know I can't ask that of Mother."

"I've already asked her."

"*What?*"

"I've already asked her, and she's already said yes. She feels this neighborhood is inappropriate—"

"*What are you trying to tell me?*"

"—for the baby," Daisy said.

*Oh, Daisy.*

"She'll *give* us the apartment, Haskell. For a *wedding present*." Daisy finally got it out.

"There's a bun in the oven, is there?" I said.

"Don't be vulgar. But yes. There is."

Of course it isn't mine, could not possibly be. Daisy *had* managed to nab me one morning, when I had a piss hard-on, unrelated to lust, and we did manage the dirty deed, somewhat. But I didn't come. Daisy, however, doesn't know this.

"Daisy. Darling. I don't see how—"

"You were drunk," Daisy said, referring to some other, fictional, time entirely. But if I had been too drunk to remember, I would have been too drunk to perform.

"I don't see how it's possible."

"Of course it's *possible*, honey." Daisy said, talking too fast, trying to pull it off. She patted her stomach. "Obviously. It's *quite* possible. You know what they say in gym class. One time will do it. Why, I know a girl who got pregnant on her very first fuck."

"Who's being vulgar now?" I said. Daisy smiled, sat down next to me, placed herself in my arms. Daisy doesn't know I faked an orgasm that morning. I haven't had one in eight or nine months, not even by myself. I could have the little bastard tissue-typed, of course. But that would be unspeakably crude, churlish, like Daisy herself, who had probably seduced me on purpose. She had probably been pregnant already, by somebody else, and slept with me that morning, for insurance, in case the *real* father, whoever he was, copped out. (Observe what television has done for my vocabulary.) But a paternity suit? My good name dragged through the mud? We'd lived together for three whole years. I had *had* her. There was no *proof* she'd deceived me. Maybe she never had.

Daisy settled herself against me and waited to be proposed to. She had never been more unattractive. She wasn't used to asking for things, she was used to demanding them. Groveling, even the subtle kind, became her not at all.

"You've known for a while, right?" I asked.

Daisy nodded.

"Why didn't you tell me?"

"I didn't want to use it unfairly. I didn't want to *force* you to marry me. And you were always so unhappy, whenever I brought it up."

"So you told Mother instead."

"Was I wrong?"

"No, not wrong. Just Daisy. Are you sure you don't want to visit Dr. Morton?" I asked. Dr. Morton was the friendly Park Avenue abortionist who had Hoovered out Daisy's womb at least once before that I knew of. I am reasonably certain the last one, now in a tissue bank somewhere, was mine, a real du Pont, pedigreed. Daisy didn't want to have it, since we were doing drugs when it was conceived, or so she claimed. She *really* didn't want to have it because she was poor then, and so was I. Daisy would never have a baby unless it could be raised by servants.

"Now that we have enough money," she said, reading my mind, "I don't see why we should wait to start a family."

"How did Mother take it?" I asked.

"Well, she was horrified at first, of course, but then she decided she liked it. She figures it'll settle you down."

"Indeed. And was this how she trapped Father?"

"Is that what you consider it? A trap?" Daisy took a deep breath. "You used to say you wanted to marry me, but you couldn't. And now that you can, you won't. You were *lying*."

"I never lie."

"What do you call it then?"

"Why do you want to marry me?" I countered.

"I love you," Daisy said.

"Yes, but why do you want to *marry* me? You have your own money now. You don't need me."

"I *want* you."

"You just want me to give in."

Earlier tonight, when Daisy came into the bedroom in a cloud of scent and sat down on the bed in her sables and satins and lifted up her demure blond hair so I could unclasp the emerald necklace, she reminded me of Mother coming into the nursery when I was small. (For most of my life, I saw Mother once a day, every evening, just before she went out for supper. I saw Father once a week, on Sundays. We played golf. He died on the eighteenth green. And that was how Daisy wanted to raise her child. Hers, for it could not possibly be mine. Like my parents raised me. Daisy didn't just want a *baby*. She wanted a baby with a trust fund.) For a second she and Mother had looked exactly alike. No wonder they were getting on so well, had so little trouble planning the rest of my life: a co-op on Park, a job with Uncle. They have a lot in common, after all. Mother is good at manipulating me, true. But Daisy is even better. Or *was*.

"I'm tired of being the girlfriend," Daisy said, as if she were getting away with it. "I'm ready to be the wife." I stroked her hair. I couldn't bear to raise a bastard sired by Vernon West, *né* Weissberg: to touch it, claim it, *name it*.

"There is some shit I will not eat," I said.

"What did you say, Haskell?" I shook my head. "Don't you love me anymore?" Daisy whined.

"Of course I love you," I said.

"You wanted to tame me. You wanted to calm me down. It was your *raison d'être*," Daisy said, mispronouncing the French.

"It's wrong, trying to change a person," I said softly.

"What did you say?"

"Wrong. I said wrong. I was wrong."

"And now that I've changed, you don't love me as much, do you?"

"You know I love you," I said. "You're the love of my life." My hands went around Daisy's neck. She tried to shrug them off. Did she sense that I couldn't stand her heat? I wondered if the baby were mine. I hoped it wasn't.

"I've got a frog in my throat, honey," were her famous last words. The frog hopped out of her mouth, away from me, into the kitchen. It's staring at me now, from under the radiator. The frog has Daisy's eyes: wary, now, but kind.

# Saturday in the Barn

Jason Mode is slow getting out of his Calvins. It's cold in the barn, too cold to be standing around naked. But that's the way Mr. Delaney wants it, and Mr. Delaney calls the shots.

Jason's flannel shirt is already off. He hangs it where Mr. Delaney tells him, on a peg near the barn door where some dead farmer, Mr. Delaney's grandfather, probably, used to hang his hat. Jason brushes his blond hair back from his eyes and glares at Mr. Delaney, who's still in his parka. But Mr. Delaney doesn't notice. He's uncoiling some electric cables, thicker than the hoses in Jason's backyard.

Jason hugs himself. "It's too cold today!" he shouts. Mr. Delaney doesn't say anything. The cables coil around his arms like snakes. When Mr. Delaney shakes free of them, they land in the straw with a soft *kerthump*. "It's freezing, Mr. Delaney. I wanna go home."

"Not yet, Jason," Mr. Delaney says absently, engrossed in making the cranky old generator come to life. "Come on, girl, come on. You can do it." The generator sputters once, then dies, but Mr. Delaney isn't discouraged. "You almost got it that time! Third time's the charm!" Mr. Delaney treats the generator like a finicky racehorse instead of the wheezing pile of junk that it is. Jason figures if they're going to come here all the time,

51

Mr. Delaney could at least buy a decent generator. One that starts when you turn it on. That's what Jason's father would do. But his father, who designs buildings in Los Angeles, wouldn't be caught dead here anyway. He would take one look at the decaying barn and have it torn down, A.S.A.P.

Jason doesn't want to think of his father. There are too many lies between them that Jason can't clear up. This morning his father stopped eating and put down his *L.A. Times*. He sat there with his spoon in his hand and a vague, confused look on his face.

"You're changing, son," his father said softly. "I'm not sure how much I like that."

Jason shrugged and gobbled his granola, which tasted like burnt cardboard all at once. He grabbed the honey bear from the center of the table and squeezed its fat plastic tummy hard. The granola still tasted like cardboard, only sweet. Jason ate it anyway, like a kid in a cereal ad.

"I must be getting old," his father said a few minutes later. Jason didn't answer. His father's spoon clinked against the cereal bowl, then stopped. After a long, deep sigh, Mr. Mode got up and left the kitchen. Jason didn't look up until his father was out of the room. He put his dishes in the sink and ran out the door, to Mr. Delaney.

Half naked, Jason puts his hands on his hips, spreads his legs wide, and sticks out his tongue defiantly at Mr. Delaney's back. The generator catches. Mr. Delaney gives a whoop of joy.

"I hate being here!" Jason yells. "I hate this place!" His hands go over his mouth automatically, but the words are already out there. They sound unnaturally loud to Jason as they echo once off the walls of the barn, hang in the air for a full second, then die.

Mr. Delaney looks up, his clown face red with anger. "What did you say, Jason?" His jowls tremble like raspberry Jell-O.

"Nothing." Jason looks at his sneakers, buried in musty straw.

"That's what I thought." Mr. Delaney smiles; Jason freezes. "You remember Molly, don't you?"

Molly was the gerbil Jason's class had adopted. Mr. Delaney cut Molly up after school one day, piece by piece, while Molly was still alive. He locked the door before he started, then pulled the shades down tight. When he started cutting, the four of them, Mr. Delaney's favorite students, tried to run away, but their teacher brought them back. Jason's father said Mr. Delaney was light on his feet for a fat man, and it was true. Mr. Delaney moved like a lizard. He caught them all easily, even Jason, who was the fastest.

Molly screamed in pain. First she had three legs, then two, then none. Jason never knew a gerbil could make so much noise. They figured Molly would get to die quicker if they did what Mr. Delaney wanted, so they stood shoulder to shoulder and forced themselves to watch. The bloody thing on the dissection table wasn't Molly by then anyway. Everyone calmed down but Ariel Bernstein, who couldn't stop sobbing. Molly was Ariel's birthday present from her grandfather in New York.

After it was over, Mr. Delaney said if any of them ever told about the new game they were going to play, the exact same thing would happen to them.

"First your daddy, then your mommy, then your brothers and sisters, and last of all, *you*!" Mr. Delaney chanted merrily. Then he explained it to them, what they had to do. Just like a geography lesson. They were fascinated despite themselves. Nothing they'd heard or read, or that their parents had told them, had prepared them, remotely, for anything like it. Mary Huong looked like she knew what was happening, but Mary had always seemed older than everybody else. At five, she had ridden a leaky boat from Vietnam with her mother and five sisters. She claimed to remember all of it, and maybe she did. Jason couldn't tell if she was lying.

"But first you get to watch," Mr. Delaney concluded. "Just like today. Just like with Molly. Does everybody understand? Are there any questions?"

The room was quiet except for Ariel's sobs, but after Mr. Delaney slapped her, Ariel calmed down.

"Does everybody understand?" he said again.

They looked at each other in confusion. Jason, who was class president, was first to speak. "Yes, Mr. Delaney," he said.

"What about the rest of you?"

"Yes, Mr. Delaney!" The little chorus was louder that time. Only Ariel didn't join in, but Mr. Delaney didn't notice. His face relaxed. He looked almost like his old self.

A few weeks after Molly died, Jason's mother let him stay up to see a movie on TV. Mrs. Mode loved films and reviewed them on the six o'clock news. Sometimes Jason watched her, but usually he didn't bother. The movie was black and white, from the 1940s, with a complicated plot Mrs. Mode admitted even she couldn't follow. Jason kept falling asleep. An hour into the movie, his mother woke him up.

"Do you know who that is?" Jason's mother asked. She pointed to a skinny teenager, washing a windshield at a gas station. He had a thin, intense face and looked bored, like Jason, and unhappy too.

"No, who?" Jason asked, not really interested. The boy didn't look like anyone he knew.

His mother laughed. "Why, that's Mr. Delaney!"

Jason didn't say anything.

"Mr. Delaney, your teacher!"

Jason got up, walked over to the television, sat down on the floor, and stared at the actor's face. The boy was nothing like Mr. Delaney.

"Did you know Mr. Delaney was a movie star once?"

"No," Jason said.

"It's true. He was. Chuckie Delaney was very famous.

He made lots of movies when he was a little boy. Dozens and dozens and dozens. Then he grew up and became a teacher.''

Are you sure that's Mr. Delaney? Jason wanted to ask. But he knew his mother never lied. He finished watching the movie, which was no longer boring because Mr. Delaney was in it.

Jason knew his mother was telling the truth for sure a few months later, at the UCLA Film Theater. Jason's father went with them. The second movie was even older than the first and had been one of his father's favorites in film school. Mr. and Mrs. Mode had seen it together, before his father had jumped ship (as Jason's mother called it) and gone into architecture.

''I've seen this just about as many times as you've seen *Roger Rabbit*,'' Mr. Mode whispered when the movie started.

Jason didn't believe it. Right away, though, he recognized Mr. Delaney, who must have been about three years old. His hair was thin and his cheeks were fat, and Mr. Delaney had a dozen chins. He was fat all over, just like now, more like himself at three than at seventeen. ''Precious'' was the word Jason's mother would have used. She used the word about things or people when they were being too cute for their own good, when she saw through them. It often popped up in her film reviews. You could tell Mr. Delaney was precious from the way he batted his eyes and mugged for the camera. The adults in the movie probably hated him, he was so precious. When the beautiful German actress, who was supposed to be his mother, had to pick Mr. Delaney up, she curled her lip and held him away from her with regal disdain. Jason spotted it right away, but his parents, all misty-eyed, holding hands, didn't notice.

''Looks like Mr. Delaney needs his diapers changed,'' Jason whispered to his father. Mr. Mode looked hard at the screen, then laughed loudly. The people in the front of them turned around and scowled. His father quieted down, but for the rest of the movie, whenever Mr. Delaney was on, Mr. Mode chuckled softly and patted Jason's hand, so Jason would know he was thinking about the diapers.

"Why did Mr. Delaney stop acting?" Jason asked his mother during the drive home.

"Nobody wanted him anymore," she said, then shrugged her shoulders. "It happens that way sometimes. It's called 'peaking early.' " Mrs. Mode let go of the steering wheel and made quote marks in the air with her hands. "Don't let it happen to you!"

"What happened to his money?"

"Oh, his wicked, greedy mother spent it all. On Cuisinarts and fur coats and . . . karate lessons!" Mrs. Mode grinned broadly.

Jason thought carefully before he spoke. All the things his mother mentioned were things she herself had.

"Guess I better not make any money then," Jason said finally. "At least until I'm older."

Mrs. Mode laughed. "I guess not, slugger. I guess you better not at that."

In April, they watched the Academy Awards. Shirley Temple was on, early in the program. She'd been one of Jason's favorites, when he was little. He had all her movies on videotape. Jason was too old now for Shirley Temple, but because of Mr. Delaney, he was interested in how she turned out.

Shirley Temple was about Mr. Delaney's age, but the resemblance stopped there. She looked nothing like herself as a child, and a lot like herself as a teenager. Jason saw her get her first screen kiss from another child actor, Dickie Moore, when she was fourteen. Both of their careers were over after that, just like Mr. Delaney's.

On TV, Shirley tried to be gracious. She held up the tiny honorary Oscar she'd received as a child. "With two of these, I could make earrings," Shirley said with a tense smile. Jason's mother told him about Shirley Temple's life, after the movies: she had married, raised a family, and been an ambassador in Africa. Shirley Temple had turned out all right. She was nothing like Mr. Delaney.

Between 1935 and 1949, Mr. Delaney made twenty-eight films. Jason went to the library and read about them. When his career ended, Mr. Delaney came home to Topanga Canyon, refurbished the family goat farm (except for the barn), and taught fifth grade in his brother-in-law's private school. His former fame endeared him to the community. Everybody in Topanga loved Mr. Delaney. All of them thought he was wonderful, including Jason's mother, who had once profiled him for *American Film* magazine.

At the Topanga School for Gifted Children, Mr. Delaney used his acting skills in various ways. He was the friendly clown at the children's parties and visited the orthopedic hospital in this costume once a month. He played Bob Cratchit in the play the sixth-graders gave at Christmas. And everyone agreed, without a doubt, that Mr. Delaney was the best Santa Claus the school had ever had.

There wasn't any need to kill Molly, not really. Even if they tell, nobody will believe them. Jason's smart enough to know that.

"One more time, children!"

"Yes, Mr. Delaney!"

"That's much better. Time to go home now." Mr. Delaney got out his big ring of keys. "Pull up the shades, Ariel." Mr. Delaney laughed merrily. "Let's get a little light on the subject!" This was one of Mr. Delaney's favorite jokes. But when Ariel didn't move, the tension crept back into his face.

"I'll do it, sir," Jason said, to head the tension off and protect Ariel. He moved toward the windows, but Mr. Delaney's big arm blocked his path.

"No. Let Ariel do it," Mr. Delaney said. There was

an awful silence. Robbie Shelton started whimpering, then stopped. They waited, all of them. Ariel finally moved. Her back was bent, her steps small and tentative. She walked like she was afraid of falling down, just like Jason's great-aunt Caroline walked before she died. Like her bones were as brittle as autumn leaves, and if she made one false move, the San Andreas fault might open up, like everybody said it was going to, and swallow her.

Ariel pulled up the shades. Sunlight flooded the classroom. Jason glanced at his Swatch: four o'clock. They had been in the classroom less than an hour. For a split second, Jason thought he might have fallen asleep, that all of it was a bad dream. Then he saw Molly in the dissecting dish, white and bloody. A single tear rolled down his cheek. He wiped it away before anybody saw. Mr. Delaney unlocked the door, opened it, and stepped outside. "I'll see all of you tomorrow morning, bright and early! Don't forget now," he said playfully. They filed out single file, like for a fire drill, staying as far away from their teacher as possible. None of them said a word. Mr. Delaney whistled as they marched. The tune echoed in the empty hallway. Delaney was a good whistler, and Jason recognized the song as one of his mother's favorite "oldies but goodies." He could almost hear her singing the words:

*"It's gonna be a bright . . . bright, sunshiny day!"*

Jason ran all the way home. By the time he got there, he felt almost normal. Both his parents were still at work in L.A. Jason poured some milk into a white plastic cup with pictures of Daffy Duck on it. He turned on the TV, but his favorite cartoons were over. Jason kicked the TV, crawled into his father's chair, and played the remote control like a toy piano. He watched the Reverend Eugene Scott, who puffed on a pipe, reminding Jason of his father, and a video by the Talking Heads, who his mother liked but his father called "noise," on MTV.

A few minutes later, Jason saw Ariel coming down the street. He and Ariel had grown up together. Sally Bernstein was his mother's best friend. They had gone to Radcliffe, where Ariel would go. Jason would go to Harvard like his father, unless he decided to play football. When he asked his father about football at Harvard, Mr. Mode laughed and shook his head. Jason might want to play football, if he got big enough. Then he would live at home and go to USC.

Jason and Ariel usually did their homework together. Then they watched TV or played games on Jason's Amiga. Sometimes they looked at his comic book collection—he had a full run of the Fantastic Four—but Ariel didn't like that much, and Jason was losing interest too. His mother told him to keep up the collection. That it would pay his tuition at Harvard.

Jason waited for Ariel. He wanted to talk to her about what happened at school. But Ariel didn't stop. Jason wondered if she was angry, because he didn't wait for her and ran home by himself, or if she was still upset over Molly. He got up and tapped on the windows, but Ariel didn't turn around. She walked like she needed an exoskeleton of steel to hold her up.

"I can't get these buttons," Jason says, fumbling with his jeans. He sticks out his lower lip, which he knows Mr. Delaney likes. A few minutes later, he's out of his Calvins, and out of his Brooks Brothers boxer shorts too, which are the same shade of blue as his father's eyes. Jason hangs the shorts on the same peg, on top of his jeans and shirt. Mr. Delaney pats Jason on the head, goes back to his equipment, and leaves Jason alone with his thoughts.

Jason wishes he could vanish like the Invisible Girl, or ignite everything he touched, like the Torch. The brittle old barn would go up in a minute, if Jason could do some of that. And half of Topanga too, he thinks. "Only *you* can prevent forest fires." Smokey the Bear came to the school last week, and Jason was impressed, even if it was just a man in a bear suit. In California, this is a bad month for fires. And it's Saturday. Both his parents are home. Their house is only three miles away.

Jason changes his fantasy. If he was big and green, like the Incredible Hulk, he could stomp Mr. Delaney into hamburger and end the stupid game with the stupid name. Mr. Delaney calls it "Naked Movie Star." Jason squirms in embarrassment whenever he says it. Mr. Delaney being precious makes him want to barf.

Thinking Mr. Delaney dead warms Jason all over. He already knows lots of ways to do it. He spends every spare minute at the public library, reading, to get ideas, and his new interest in books delights his parents, who think Jason watches too much TV. They wouldn't be so happy if they knew what he was reading, Jason thinks, a little guiltily: Agatha Christie, Ross Macdonald, and Patricia Highsmith. Highsmith, especially. Jason usually skims the characters and descriptions and gets straight to the good parts, the murders. But sometimes he gets carried away by the story. Then he reads the book straight through.

Jason knows it's too dangerous to try anything yet, that his plans aren't perfect. Mr. Delaney might survive, and Jason doesn't want his dog, Samantha, to end up like Robbie Shelton's cat, traces of whom were found in Robbie's backyard the day after Robbie missed a date with Mr. Delaney. Mr. and Mrs. Shelton think a coyote got her, but Robbie knows better. The Monday after Tory died, her photograph was gone from the Pet Bulletin Board. When his parents bought a Persian kitten for him, Robbie made them give it away.

Jason loves Samantha, but he knows Samantha is just a dog. And since Mr. Delaney is a coward—only cowards pick on things weaker than themselves, his father taught him—Jason isn't afraid for his parents. Mr. Delaney would never mess with another adult, and Jason is an only child.

Mr. Delaney will be dead soon, and all his creepy friends with him, the ones he brings around to play the

game, or watch it. Jason is confident of that. Then maybe
Ariel will start talking, get out of the hospital, and come
back to school where she belongs. Ariel isn't crazy, like
everybody says. She's smart, even smarter than Jason,
though it's sort of hard to believe that now, looking at
her. But when Jason went to see her at the hospital and
whispered in her ear that he knew her secret, Ariel looked
up and smiled at him. At least Jason thinks she smiled.
Ariel has a horse, three cats, and a baby sister. They're
safe, as long as Ariel is in the hospital. Ariel isn't crazy.
She just doesn't want to play.

When the bright white lights come on, part of Jason
winces, but another part of him is relaxed. The lights,
which look so cold, warm him immediately. His goose
pimples disappear. His teeth stop chattering. Mr. Delaney turns, proud of himself, and smiles at Jason fondly.

"Just one more second, tiger." He fiddles with the
automatic timer on the video camera. "I'll warm you up
soon enough." Mr. Delaney thinks Jason really likes
him. Jason's a better actor than Mr. Delaney ever was.

Jason waits. The game will start soon, and then it will
be over. Too much time has already been wasted. Saturday morning is almost gone. He'll make the game end
quickly. Jason can do that now, though he couldn't at the
beginning. Then he'll go home and play with Samantha.
Maybe he'll ride his bike to the library for one of the
Patricia Highsmiths he still hasn't read, or to the hospital
to see Ariel. Then he'll play Adventure and watch cartoons.

Anticipation carries Jason through the next ten minutes, the length of the magazine on the camera. When he
gets home, both his parents are sitting in the living room.
They tell him right away that Ariel is dead. She walked
out of the hospital, down to the San Diego Freeway and
onto the off ramp. Jason's mother looks at him and bursts
into tears. Jason goes straight to his room.

A few minutes later, his father taps on the door. Does
Jason want to talk? Jason doesn't answer. His father tip-

toes away. Jason telephones Mary Huong, to tell her about Ariel. At first Mary sounds sorry, but when Jason mentions Mr. Delaney and the game, Mary's voice changes. She acts like she doesn't know what Jason's talking about. A few seconds later she hangs up. Robbie Shelton would be no help at all. Since his cat disappeared, most of her, Robbie's hardly even there. Jason wonders if Mr. Delaney's picked someone out to take Ariel's place.

Jason goes downstairs. In the living room, his mother cries with big hopeless sobs. His father strokes his mother's hair.

"There, there, Edith," Jason hears him say in his softest voice. "There, there, my darling. There, there."

Jason goes into the kitchen and gets a knife out of the silverware drawer, like he's hypnotized. But once it's in his hand, he doesn't know what to do with it. It isn't a very sharp knife. Jason sits down at the kitchen table and cleans his fingernails. He picks up the honey bear and pokes its plastic snout. The mouth stays closed.

"Here comes the airplane," he says in Mr. Delaney's voice. Then he slits the honey bear's throat.

# Wild America

Welcome to WILD AMERICA! Do you need instructions?

YES

You are living in the richest kingdom in the world, where others have found fame and fortune, though it is rumored that some who enter here are never heard from again. Where would you like to begin your adventure?

Indicate choice:

BEVERLY HILLS

You must be joking!
Indicate choice:

GROSSE POINTE

You must be joking!
Indicate choice:

DETROIT

OK

You are a thirty-year-old *auto* worker in *Detroit, Michigan*. Ten years ago you married a fellow worker. You now have two children. A year ago, your factory closed. Neither you nor your spouse were able to find other employment. Your unemployment insurance has run out. Although your savings are gone, you do not qualify for welfare. You've already sold your lakeside cabin. Now the bank is threatening to take away your house, the car dealership to repossess your car, and the furniture store to confiscate all your furniture, including the TV set. To top it off, your baby needs an operation!

You may now begin your adventure. I will be your eyes and hands. Direct me with commands of one or two words. If you need help type HELP. To see how you're doing type SCORE.


\*\*\*\*\*\*\*\*\*\*\*\*GOOD LUCK\*\*\*\*\*\*\*\*\*\*\*\*


You are standing in front of a white frame house in a working-class neighborhood in *Detroit, Michigan*.
You are wearing:
  jeans
  T-shirt
  sneakers
You are carrying:
  nothing
  There is a shiny Chrysler here!
  There is a white motorboat here!
  There is a new Schwinn bicycle here!


GO IN


You are inside a cheerful living room, with exits to the east, west, and south.
  There is a GE color television here!
  There is a leatherette wallet here!
  There is a gleaming crib here!

The crib contains:
  bouncing baby!

GET WALLET

OK

OPEN WALLET

The wallet contains:
  MasterCard
  Visa
  pawn ticket

GO SOUTH

You're in a kitchen with yellow wallpaper.
  There is a sparkling Frigidaire here!
  There is a Maytag washer-dryer here!

OPEN FRIDGE

The refrigerator contains:
  dog food

OPEN WASHING MACHINE

The washing machine contains:
  dirty diapers

GO NORTH

You're in the living room.
Suddenly an enraged spouse enters from the door to the
west and tells you to get the hell out, you deadbeat!

GET TV

The spouse jumps in front of the TV and screams, "Over my dead body!"

KILL SPOUSE

With what, your bare hands?

· YES

Congratulations! You have just killed a *spouse* with your bare hands! (Amazing, isn't it!)

GET TV

OK

GET BABY

The baby appears to be afraid of you and cries when you pick it up.

SHUT BABY UP

The bouncing baby cries and cries. It is making you a nervous wreck!

KILL BABY

With what, your bare hands?

YES

Congratulations! You have just killed a *baby* with your bare hands! (Amazing, isn't it!)

GO WEST

You are in a small blue bedroom, with exits to the east and south.

    There is freshly waxed furniture here!

    There is an alligator purse here!

GET PURSE

OK

OPEN PURSE

The purse contains:
    keys
    red lipstick
    pistol

GET KEYS

OK

GET PISTOL

OK

DROP PURSE

OK

GO NORTH

You're in the bedroom.

GO EAST

You're in the living room.
    There is a dead spouse here!
    There is a gleaming crib here!

The crib contains:
 dead baby

GO EAST

You're outside the house.
 There is a shiny Chrysler here!
 There is a white motorboat here!
 There is a new Schwinn bicycle here!

GO CAR

You are now sitting in the car.

START CAR

The car refuses to start.

USE KEYS

When you place your key in the ignition, the car turns over once or twice, then stops. The gas gauge reads EMPTY.

GET OUT

OK

WALK

You can't walk around carrying a *TV* in *Detroit*! The police will arrest you!

GET BICYCLE

Your ten-year-old child jumps out from behind a bush and prevents you from taking the bicycle.

KILL CHILD

With what, your bare hands?

YES

The child is too fast for you and manages to get on the bicycle and ride away, screaming for help.

USE PISTOL

By the time you get out your pistol, the child is already out of range.

GO NORTH

You're in front of a billboard that says MCFLEECEM TECH-NICAL SCHOOL: TRAIN FOR A NEW CAREER! CALL 888-8888!! There is a phone booth in front of the billboard.

GO PHONE BOOTH

A large agitated gentleman emerges from the phone booth and asks if you'd like a taste of something.

YES

The gentleman asks if you have any money.

NO

The gentleman shrugs meaningfully and points to your TV set.

DROP TV

The gentleman smiles, hands you a small white packet, picks up your TV, and walks away.

OPEN PACKET

The packet contains:
  cheap cocaine

DO COCAINE

You immediately feel better, sort of.

GO EAST

You're standing in front of a dingy pawnshop. A bum is sitting in front of the door asleep. The bum is holding a battered fedora. In the fedora is a mysterious envelope. Written on the envelope are the magic words CHIMERA TRAVEL: YOUR TICKET IS ENCLOSED.

GET HAT

When you reach for the hat, an enormous dog comes out from behind the building and begins to growl ominously.

KILL DOG

With what, your bare hands?

YES

I wouldn't try that if I were you.

SHOOT DOG

You can't do that yet.

USE PISTOL

In order to shoot, you need bullets.

GO PAWNSHOP

You're inside the pawnshop, a room packed with merchandise of *ALL* descriptions. At the east end of the room is the cage. A pawnbroker is inside the cage, watching you warily.

GO EAST

The pawnbroker asks you what you want. He is fingering something hidden under the counter, which is liable to be a big shotgun!

DROP TICKET

The pawnbroker takes the ticket and asks for $20.

DROP PISTOL

In exchange for your pistol, the pawnbroker gives you another ticket and then produces a shiny jewelry box!

GET TICKET

OK

GET BOX

OK

OPEN BOX

The box refuses to open.

USE KEYS

I see no keys here. Perhaps they're in your Chrysler! Ha!

GO OUT

You're in front of the pawnshop.
  There is a sleeping bum here!
  There is an enormous dog here!

GO WEST

You're at the billboard.

GO DRUG DEALER

A large agitated gentleman emerges from the phone booth
and asks if you have any money.

NO

The gentleman shrugs his shoulders meaningfully.

TRUST ME

The gentleman says, "No dice."

GO SOUTH

You're at the intersection of two streets, where everything looks alike. A police car whizzes by you, sirens
screaming. To the south you can hear ambulances, more
police cars, and great commotion!

GO EAST

You're at the south entrance to a small park. A cheerful
senior citizen is coming out of the park, carrying the
proceeds of a church bake sale in a small canvas bag.

GET BAG

The cheerful senior citizen refuses to relinquish the bag.

KILL SENIOR CITIZEN

With what? Your bare hands?

YES

Congratulations! You have just killed a *scnior citizen*
with your bare hands! (Amazing, isn't it!)

GET BAG

OK

OPEN BAG

The bag contains:
  $72.50

GET MONEY

OK

DROP BAG

OK

GO WEST

You're at the intersection.

GO NORTH

You're at the billboard.

GO DRUG DEALER

A large agitated gentleman emerges from the phone booth and asks if you have any money.

DROP MONEY

The gentleman takes your money, hands you a small white packet, and walks away.

DO COCAINE

I see no cocaine here.

OPEN PACKET

The packet contains:
  baking soda

GO WEST

You're at the pawnshop.

GO IN

You're inside the pawnshop.

GO CAGE

You're standing in front of the pawnbroker.

DROP TICKET

The pawnbroker demands $30 in exchange for the ticket.

DROP MONEY

The pawnbroker gives you a small pistol.

BUY BULLETS

I see no bullets here.

GO OUT

You're outside the pawnshop.

GO EAST

You're standing in front of a small frame building with guns in the window. A brightly colored sign outside proclaims BIG AL'S.

GO IN

You're inside Big Al's Friendly Gun Store. At the south end of the room, Big Al is watching you warily.

GO SOUTH

You're standing in front of the proprietor, Big Al.

BUY BULLETS

Big Al demands $10 for a box of bullets.

DROP MONEY

Big Al hands you a small box of bullets and bids you a cheerful good day.

GO OUT

You're in front of the gun store.

LOAD GUN

Your gun is now loaded.

DROP JEWELRY BOX

OK

SHOOT JEWELRY BOX

The jewelry box flies open! It contains:
  tarnished wedding ring

DROP RING

You aren't carrying it.

GO WEST

You're in front of the pawnshop.

SHOOT DOG

I see no dog here.

GET TICKET

I see no ticket here.

LOOK!

You're in front of the pawnshop. A sign on the window
says CLOSED FOR THE DAY.

GO EAST

You're in front of the gun store.

GO EAST

You're at the north entrance of a small park.

GO SOUTH

You're in the park, with exits in \*ALL\* directions. There is an attractive member of the opposite sex sitting on a bench nearby. The person waves to you and smiles invitingly.

GO BENCH

You're standing in front of the bench. Up close, the person is even more alluring.

SIT BENCH

You're on the bench. The attractive member of the opposite sex looks deep into your eyes and asks you if you'd like to party.

YES

The attractive person asks if you have any money.

DROP MONEY

The attractive person pulls out a pair of handcuffs and clamps them on you, before you have time to react. Oh, dear! You have just solicited an undercover cop!

SHOOT COP

You can't shoot! You're handcuffed!

RUN

Run where?

RUN SOUTH

You're at the south entrance of the park.
   There is a dead senior citizen here!
   There is an empty canvas bag here!

RUN

   There is no place left to run. You're surrounded by police!

SURRENDER

OK


*Hands behind the fucking head.*
*Easy. He's clean.*
*Lemme dance with him, Charlie.*
*Forget it.*
*See if he knows the cha-cha.*
*Just read him his rights.*
*Awright, awright. "You have the right to remain silent" . . . FOREVER!*
*Orville . . .*
*Just a joke.*
*You been telling it a solid year!*
*That's because it's so funny. Maniac cop! Kaboom!*
*Put a lid on it, you two. Fucking Laurel and Hardy over there. Did you see Slotnik's face when she heard she got a Code 3 in her johnny trap?*
   *"Anything you say can and will be used against you in a court of law. You have the right to an attorney."*
*Nearly pissed her little panties.*
   *"If you cannot afford an attorney one will be provided for you. Do you understand these rights?"*
*The nice man asked you a question.*
*What's your opinion on Slotnik? Does she spit, do you think? Or does she swallow?*
*ANSWER THE FUCKING QUESTION, SCUMBAG!*

YES

You are engulfed in a cloud of greasy black exhaust. Choking and gagging from carbon monoxide fumes, you emerge to find yourself in front of an immense gray building. The words *WAYNE COUNTY COURTHOUSE* are chiseled above the entrance. The police push you roughly inside. You're in the courthouse, with passages off in *ALL* directions.

There is an overworked public defender here!

There are several copies of the Yale Law Review here!

HELP

I know of places, events, and things: a set of keys in an alligator purse, a gas can hidden in a motorboat. Usually people who have trouble moving just need to try a few more words. If you kiss the spouse, for example (KISS SPOUSE) it immediately calms down. If you wash the diapers (WASH DIAPERS) the spouse allows you to take the TV set. The baby stops crying if you burp it. Feed the dog and it goes away. Hint for beginners: If you kill too many people early in the game, you may have trouble moving later on (but not necessarily).

Enter Command.

PLEA BARGAIN

OK

SCORE

You scored 10 out of a possible 81134500. That makes you a *MENACE TO SOCIETY*! Better luck next time! Want to try again? In ten to twenty years? With time off for good behavior? Ha!

FUCK YOU

Swearing is not permitted.
Answer the question!

YES

OK, long time no see.

Welcome to WILD AMERICA!

# Ken Kesey Day

Like everybody else at Reed College, I had read *The Electric Kool-Aid Acid Test*, so when Ken Kesey Day came at last, I was ready. After breakfast, my roommate Susie Floyd and I dropped acid, Orange Sunshine, which had arrived in Susie's mailbox the day before from her boyfriend in San Diego, taped inside a copy of *Been Down So Long It Looks Like Up to Me*. Then we went back to the dorm to dress.

Both of us had scrimped to buy floor-length velvet gowns at a thrift shop in downtown Portland, Susie because her parents hated Reed and wouldn't give her any money, me because my parents didn't have any money to give. If Susie hadn't dragged me to a record store where I distracted the clerk while Susie walked out with seventeen Jefferson Airplane albums under her USC football jersey which we sold outside Commons for two dollars a pop, I wouldn't have been able to buy the dress at all, but she did. Susie was the best shoplifter on campus. I never bought a book while we lived together, but because Reed had an honor system, and stealing from our bookstore might result in increased tuition, which I couldn't afford, I made Susie hitch downtown to Portland State to steal them.

Susie and I wanted to look good for Ken Kesey. He might spot one of us and pick us up in his burly ex-wrestler's arms and carry us away on the Magic Bus to his farm in eastern Oregon, where we would get stoned every day and talk about . . . whatever. Then Ken would write for a few hours while we embroidered flowers on his bell-bottoms or did macramé or strung beads or baked hash brownies or, in my case, painted. Later, we would help him make the yummy, all-natural yogurt he sold under the Contented Cow label. For Ken Kesey, we would even *milk* the cows. Probably we would.

One of us might become Ken Kesey's old lady! Stranger things had happened. The year before, two religion majors ran away with the Living Theater, like little boys used to run away with the circus. After the performance, they couldn't bear to put their clothes back on. And a girl in Kalispell, Montana, where I grew up, ran away with the Electric Flag. Gail Lindstrom left town in the dead of night, with just the clothes on her back (blue-and-white striped bell-bottoms, tie-dyed T-shirt, and fringed white leather jacket, exactly like Sly Stone's) and was *never heard from again*, which gave the Kalispell PTA some much-needed ammunition in their never-ending fight to control their would-be wayward daughters. (I tried to be a groupie once, when I was fourteen. I went backstage after a Buffalo Springfield concert. Stephen Stills, who, at close range, was an adult, a *grown man*, and not a very cute one at that, smiled at me. In the hallway of the Ramada Inn, where I followed him, he kissed me. He *put his tongue in my mouth*. I fled.) I wondered if Gail Lindstrom was all right. I hoped she was.

My gown was burgundy. Susie's was royal blue. The colors were pulsing merrily. Susie put the new Band album on the stereo. We wielded bright lipsticks, made up our eyes, and ironed each other's hair. Susie painted a tiny spider on my cheek with black eyeliner, to hide a mole I was self-conscious of. We complimented each other extravagantly, then went outside.

There was a giant white balloon on the lawn. We

crawled through a tunnel to get inside. Susie brought bubbles to blow. She dipped her wand in the tiny jar and waved.

"Bubbles . . . *inside the bubble*," Susie said. This seemed incredibly profound at the time.

"Far out," I said. Susie was more advanced, philosophically, than I was, since she was from California. The sparkling bubbles wafted down. I reached out and touched one. It popped.

"Oooooh, don't kill it," Susie commanded. She was more spiritual too. Far be it from me to slaughter a bubble. Susie whirled away in an incandescent cloud, blue dress shining, black hair billowing out. People watched her and applauded. I sat down on the floor of the balloon to sulk, then got up immediately. The floor was sticky with soapy water. I didn't want to ruin the velvet.

"Do you get the feeling we're being *watched*?" Susie said, after she was out of bubble goop. She was getting that look again, that anxious look. I knew it *so* well.

"You're beautiful. You're blowing bubbles. Of course people are watching you," I said, cross and jealous.

"Do you think I'm getting paranoid? Am I?" she said. Susie never could handle her acid, although she was much braver than me in her choice of drop points: department store escalators, crowded beaches, shopping malls. My favorite Susie-on-acid story involved a sleeping bag, a boyfriend, and Pasadena the night before the Rose Bowl parade. Her favorite Ellen-on-acid story took place right here, in the chapel, when the Film Society showed *M* without subtitles and I swore I could understand the German.

As Susie and I walked outside, hand in hand, a film crew followed us. The camera said CBS on its side.

"We *are* being watched," I told Susie, pointing to the men. "Look. You're not getting paranoid at all."

"Oooooh, the media!" Susie squealed like a stepped-on

rat, raised a tiny fist in the air, jumped up and down, and shrieked, "The whole world is watching! The whole world is watching!" The cameraman didn't stop filming. The sound man held out his microphone to catch every word of Susie's chant.

"What's this for?" I asked the guy with the mike, who wore a navy blue suit and a red bow tie.

"The six o'clock news," he said.

"The *national* news?" On Westmoreland Drive, a garishly painted school bus chugged up the hill.

The cameraman tugged on the mike wielder's arm. "Get out the shotgun, Eddie," he said. Susie jumped twenty feet. I calmed her down with difficulty. The cameraman laughed till he cried.

"The mike!" Eddie said, rummaging in his equipment bag. "The shotgun *mike*. You thought he meant . . . oh, dear. Haw, haw, haw."

"Some fun," I said.

Eddie plugged a foam-covered magic wand into his tape recorder. "That's right, girls! Walter Cronkite!" he tossed over his shoulder as he trotted toward the bus, which was passing the library.

"*That's* not Walter Cronkite," Susie whispered.

"Of course it's not," I said, squeezing her hand.

Then, with an evil grin on his aging face, Eddie turned back to us and yelled, "Tonight, at six o'clock, no matter where they live, *your parents are gonna be watching you.*"

This put Susie over the edge into total and complete acid paranoia. "My parents?" she screeched. "Oh, no!" But Eddie was already far away, guffawing at his great wit.

Susie grabbed my arm and followed him. "Not my parents! My parents can't see me like this! Don't we have to sign a—a *release* or something?"

"He's just bullshitting," I said, dragging my feet. "I don't think he was from the national news at all."

"They'll take me out of school, Ellen. They're just

looking for an excuse. They never wanted me to come here. They think Reed is all Communists and hippies. They think it was founded by *John* Reed.''

''Wasn't it?'' I deadpanned. Susie's parents were so sure Reed was a commie drug den they wouldn't send her any money. They were afraid she'd buy drugs. Instead, they opened accounts for her at all the swank stores, where Susie charged my art supplies and the other necessities she couldn't steal, sold them to me for a fraction of their actual price, and bought drugs, though most of the time you didn't have to *buy* drugs. I myself had never actually bought drugs. That seemed uncool, somehow. If you were a girl, you didn't have to. People gave them to you.

''Calm down, Susie. Think about it a minute.'' The camera crew was halfway across the lawn. The Magic Bus passed Eliot Circle.

''Now *I'm* a hippie,'' Susie wailed.

''Listen, do you really think Walter Cronkite cares about Ken Kesey Day? I mean, really, really *cares*, with all that's going on in the world?'' If Susie was more advanced philosophically, I was more *political*.

Susie stopped walking. ''I guess not,'' she said.

''*Of course* he doesn't. And if we're on the local news, so what? That'll be fun, won't it?''

Susie brightened. ''We'll be like *movie stars*. Everyone will *see* us. It'll be far out!'' Then anxiously: ''Does my hair look all right?'' I said it did. ''What about my pupils?'' Susie stared at me. Her eyes were black craters with tiny blue rims.

''Fine,'' I lied. ''How about mine?''

''Oh, yours are fine,'' she said with an airy wave of her hand, not even bothering to look. ''Yours are *always* fine.'' Susie envied my eyes, which are yellow, like my hair, and disinclined to show my feelings. (''Your eyes are so *cool*,'' Susie said often.) People called us Snow White and Rose Red. ''I wish I had your coloring,'' Susie said. ''Maybe they'd call me *Pink*

Floyd!'' Susie making a joke was more or less always pathetic. Then, looking thoughtful, also a pitiful sight: "Six o'clock. That's a long time. That'll be hard to remember.''

"I'll remember for both of us."

"Okay!"

"Now let's go see Ken!"

"Bitchin'!'' Susie said, forgetting she was a hippie, not a surfer girl anymore. With Ken Kesey—a great man, an artist, a *genius*, one of *us*—it wouldn't be like being a groupie at all, or so we thought, as we tripped across the lawn. It wouldn't be just sex, which, in any case, we had already had. If one of us was lucky, it would be *love*. True love. With somebody famous *and* brilliant, every smart girl's dream, even better than a rock star. I said it would be Susie, since she was prettier; since I was smarter and Ken was an intellectual, Susie said it would be me. I laughed. I knew more about intellectuals than Susie did. It wasn't usually brains they went for, though having brains didn't always hurt. I had a pair of rose-colored granny glasses in my tiny beaded purse. I put them on. The Magic Bus stopped in front of the old dorm block. We picked up our skirts and ran.

Ken Kesey was already out of the bus when we arrived. He was talking to our local wrestling champ, Owen Millsap, a sophomore. Ken Kesey was dressed exactly like Owen: T-shirt, faded Levi's, old cowboy boots, silver belt buckle. But, unlike Owen, he had a very pretty woman on his arm who looked like she belonged there. It would be very difficult, I thought sadly, to dislodge her from that arm. She had a death grip on it. Her floor-length tie-dyed caftan looked expensive, like silk. When she opened her mouth to laugh at one of Ken's jokes, her big smile glittered: her left front tooth was gold, set with a tiny ruby. She wore a green-and-yellow parrot on her shoulder, the way girls at home used to wear live lizards with tiny collars, attached to their sweaters by gold circle pins. But the lizards were always committing suicide. They were always shouting "Geronimo!", diving off those sweaters, and breaking their tiny necks. Lizards pinned to sweaters was a very brief fad in Kalispell. I hoped nothing like that happened to Ken Kesey's girlfriend's parrot.

Susie and I stared at the woman, then at each other, crushed again.

"And that's the way it is, on October 15, 1970," I said in my very best Walter Cronkite voice.

Susie giggled. "So it goes," she said. Susie loved Kurt Vonnegut. Back home in San Diego she had a white cat named Ice-9.

"He's awfully old, isn't he?" she said dismissively of Ken Kesey, who had taken his T-shirt off in preparation for the event of the year, the big wrestling match between Reed and the Farm. I nodded. Ken Kesey was on the plump side too. It had been a long time since he'd been heavyweight champion of Oregon. Some of that heavy weight had sagged. And his teeth were not among the whitest, despite all the milk he no doubt drank. But his girlfriend, or wife, or whatever she was, was really incredibly pretty. Prettier than Susie, much prettier than me, even if she was older, but then so was Ken Kesey.

Ken Kesey sat down on the grass and stuck his legs out, one at a time. His girlfriend bent over and pulled off his cowboy boots. The parrot squawked and dug its claws into her shoulder. Ken Kesey had holes in his socks. When the woman straightened up, the parrot shat on her caftan. Ken Kesey won the wrestling match, but some people said that was because Owen Millsap was just being nice.

"He's really cute, isn't he?" Susie said, transferring her attention to Owen, the graceful loser, all at once. I shrugged. Owen was from Idaho, much too close to Montana to have any appeal for me. When I arrived at the Portland airport, he was the one assigned to meet me—to make me feel at home, he explained in the car while I fidgeted in misery. Owen was the kind of boy who volunteered for things like that. A real good Scout, with school spirit. In his spare time, he shoed horses like the boys back home, the ones I was trying so hard to get away from. When I saw him standing there, holding a sign with my name on it, I almost went back to Montana. But for Susie, raised on surfers, Owen was quite the exotic. He didn't smoke, not even cigarettes. I wondered if Susie would be able to corrupt him, then made some excuse and left her to it. Owen had his eyes on Susie's breasts, which were formidable. When Susie caught him staring at her and met his eyes, Owen blushed. I felt sorry for him.

I walked around the old dorm block. Everybody looked like I did, with velvet and paisley and fringes and painted faces. All the dogs wore red or blue bandannas and had names like Oxomoxo and Che. Three tripping philosophy majors got up off the lawn and followed me, mesmerized by my dress.

"Can we touch it?" one of them asked. "Is it cool?" It wasn't, but I said it was. They petted the dress like it was alive and I wasn't.

I got tired of being stroked and made my way back to the bus, but Susie was gone, like everybody else. The door to the bus was open. I climbed in. The Magic Bus smelled like pot, parrot shit, sour yogurt, and sex. Maybe some Merry Prankster had thrown up in there too. I sat in the driver's seat, where Neal Cassady used to sit, before he pranked his last. We have the same last name, but we aren't related. Sometimes I tell people we are. They *believe* me.

I heard a noise behind me and jumped up. There was a Merry Prankster, three rows back, scratching himself and yawning. He was extremely fat. His skin was pockmarked. His hair was matted and gray. He noticed me,

smiled. He had a number of missing teeth, like that Hog
Farm guy, Hugh Romney, in *Woodstock*.

"You wanna ball?" he said. I shook my head. The
man looked all pranked out, but I couldn't know that for
certain. I backed off the bus, holding my hands out, palms
up, as if to a strange, maybe rabid dog. The man scooted
across his seat, leaned out the window, and smiled like
a jack-o'-lantern. What is it about being a hippie that
makes your teeth fall out? I wondered. Did I say this out
*loud*? If I did, it was an accident. I didn't mean to. The
man gave me the finger anyway. "You little bitch," he
said.

The dinner bell rang. I wasn't hungry, but I walked to
Commons. Maybe Susie, my only friend, would be there,
though I doubted it. She probably had Owen hogtied by
then, branded. When I got to the door, I noticed my
shoes were in my hand, where my purse used to be. The
purse was probably still on the bus, under the driver's
seat. I wasn't going back there, not alone. I sat down on
the steps in front of Commons and tried to put my shoes
on, but it was complicated. They were Greek sandals,
very impractical for October, with lots of delicate straps
and laces and things, and when I tried to deal with them,
I found I was more stoned than I thought. I couldn't
cope. I couldn't hold my acid. I giggled. I stood up and
walked into Commons barefoot, which was strictly
against the rules, a Health Department violation, but
maybe since half the student body was tripping, nobody
would even notice.

"Don't move!" somebody said as I walked through
the double doors, nabbed.

It didn't take them long at all to catch me. How amazing. I thought I was luckier than *that*. I wondered what
the penalty was, for walking into Commons barefoot.
Going to bed without supper? Sunlight was streaming in
through the skylight, hitting me full in the face. I reached
up and shaded my eyes.

"I said, don't *move*."

A boy walked up the steps and stood next to me. He took my hand away from my face. He was the best-looking boy I'd ever seen, except on television.

"You've got wonderful eyes," he said. "Like a tiger. Are they always that color, or is it the sun?"

"I don't know," I said, squinting up at him. He was big and broad-shouldered, not wasted at all, like most artists, intellectuals, and geniuses. His hair was dark and short. He carried a briefcase. He *shaved*. "I can't see them. What color are they?"

"Kind of a yellow gold. Sun-colored."

"They're always that color," I said proudly. He tilted my face up toward him and examined it.

"Nose, okay. Hair, nice. Skin, very nice. Eyes, *very* nice. Mouth—" He kissed me hard. He shoved his tongue so far back in my mouth I almost gagged, but I didn't pull away. When he let me go, I almost fell over. "Very, *very* nice. You should do something about those ears—"

"What, have them bobbed?" I said, recovering. "Like a Doberman?"

"—but on the whole, I think you'll do. Freshman?"

"Uh huh."

"Tripping your brains out?"

"You bet."

"I never take drugs."

"Why not?" Everybody I knew took drugs of some sort, except for my dorm mommy, Juanita Kazin, the only person at Reed who bothered to join Mensa.

"I don't like losing control," he said. I had no idea what he was talking about. I *loved* losing control. Then: "I'm Rick Lansky."

"I know." Rick looked pleased at being recognized. He was a painter, the best on campus. I'd seen him once or twice before, from a distance, in the old bus garage where the studios were. "I'm Ellen," I said. I was a painter too, or trying to be. But Rick didn't say he knew me.

What he said was, "Hi, Ellen." Then he opened the door I'd just come through and held it for me politely. When I didn't move fast enough, he snapped his fingers.

"Come on," Rick said. I came.

I don't remember much about the party we went to. I remember coming down off the acid. I remember having far too much Gallo Hearty Burgundy. I remember spaghetti, and a sauce made out of peanuts. Before the dinner started, formally, I scooped a little bit of the sauce out of the bowl with my fingers. Rick saw me and shook his head. Maybe I wouldn't do after all. I remember sitting at the dinner table and hearing a Greek man say I was talking too much, though I hardly talked at all, but the Greek said I had interrupted him once too often, and Rick looked at me like I wasn't worth the trouble, and then there was me, dragging Rick into the bathroom and kissing him and saying, "Please, please, please, please, please, please, *please*." Rick took my hand and put it on his crotch.

We went back into the dining room, where I apologized to the Greek for interrupting him. "Beautiful girls should be seen and not heard," he said magnanimously. Rick nodded. I could see it made him happy to hear another man call me beautiful. When we left, the Greek kissed me. He had peanut butter in his mustache.

"Where do you live?" Rick said, after he gave me my purse. We were standing in front of the Magic Bus. The Merry Prankster was gone, unfortunately. I wanted Rick to wipe the floor with him.

"Foster three," I said. My shoes were on my feet again. I remember Rick kneeling down to lace them up, then putting his head under my dress. But once he got it up there, he didn't do anything.

"Ugly, ugly, ugly," Rick said, and he was right. Foster was the ugliest dorm on campus. It was new and modern. It wasn't covered with ivy, like the old dorm block. But I had never complained about my room. I was on scholarship, lucky to be at Reed, fortunate to live anywhere.

"I'm sorry," I said.

"I have an eight o'clock. We'll stay at your place."

"I think we should wait," I said feebly, before he took my clothes off.

Rick said, "Why wait for anything, when you can have it right now?"

Later, in my narrow monastic bed, Rick and I discussed my education. Rick talked. I listened.

"There's only two things a chick needs to learn," Rick said. "You're not a libber, are you, Ellen?"

I shook my head vigorously. It was social suicide, being a libber. The boys called the libbers "dykes."

Rick smiled. "How to cook and how to fuck." I was shocked Rick would use the word while we were doing it. "Do you know how to cook?" I nodded. "If you're rich," Rick said, "you don't even need to know that. But you're not rich, are you?" I shook my head. Rick rammed into me.

"A chick's gotta be good in bed. That's her *job*, okay? Like a cat's gotta eat birds, and a dog's gotta chase rabbits." I had no idea whether or not I was good in bed. I suspected I wasn't. What did it mean, anyway? I didn't know, and I didn't know how to find out. Rick was still inside me, still talking when I fell asleep.

When I woke up the next morning, Rick was sitting at my desk with his briefcase open, studying. He noticed I was awake, put down his pencil, came over to the bed, and kissed me. His mouth was sour and so was mine. He took off his jeans and got under the covers. I started to fake an orgasm, like I had the night before. Rick told me not to bother.

Afterward, Rick said, "Billy Roth told me you were a nice little piece. He didn't tell me *how* nice."

"He . . . *told* you?" I finally got out. I had slept with Billy Roth once, during Orientation Week, and had regretted it.

Rick laughed. "You weren't going to pretend to be a virgin, now, were you?" I was. I usually pretended, more or less, to be a virgin.

While Rick showered, I looked through his books. All of them were about psychology.

"Will you raise your kids in a Skinner box?" I said pertly, when he came back.

"I'm not having kids," Rick said. I watched him dress. He seemed more like a man than a boy.

Rick had a car, a Mercedes, the color of dried blood. I had never been in a car like that. I had never even seen one up close. Rick cut his eight o'clock and took me downtown to the Benson Hotel for breakfast, then drove me back to campus. He pulled the Mercedes into a no-parking zone, right in front of Eliot Hall, and kissed me. My Humanities professor, Dr. Spargo, walked by and raised an eyebrow. He frowned. I couldn't tell whether he was frowning at me, for being with Rick and kissing him in public, or at the car, which he could never afford on an assistant professor's salary. I liked Dr. Spargo. I was sorry he saw me sitting there.

Susie came in the next afternoon, purring like a contented cat. I started babbling about Rick and how great he was. Susie was thrilled that I'd finally gotten a boyfriend, but she cut me off in mid-gush and made me get to the good part.

"So did you have one?" she asked.

"One what?"

"*You* know," she said, raising an eyebrow. Oh. An orgasm. Neither of us understood what orgasms *were*, for girls, and neither did the boys we slept with, or if they did they never let on, but Susie and I discussed them at length, trying to figure out what they were and how to have them. We bought a copy of Masters and Johnson, but even Susie, with all her experience, couldn't bring herself to try the things they suggested.

"Ask a boy to *what*? Ugh!" she'd say. "I'd sooner be boiled in oil."

"I don't know," I said. "Did you?"

"I don't know. He was so *quick*." I laughed. I could've told Susie that yesterday. Owen could probably be retrained with effort. But Susie didn't have that much patience. Owen wouldn't last two weeks.

Rick didn't call. I didn't expect him to. But three days later, he came to my studio. I was painting something political, about racism in the South. Rick looked at my painting compassionately, or so I thought. Then he said, pointing to one of the jeering rednecks, "Where did you get this color, Ellen? Out of a tube marked FLESH?"

Rick grabbed my arm and turned it over. He squeezed several blobs of color onto my arm. He mixed the paint and applied it with deft strokes to my canvas.

"Black skin has a lot of colors in it," he said, pointing to the corpse, swinging from a tree. "It isn't just black. There's a lot of blue there." I held my arm out and kept it still. Ten minutes later, the painting was a million times better. The people looked like people. The skin looked like skin.

"It's not your fault," Rick said after I'd wiped my eyes and vowed I'd never paint again and heard Rick say that was a good idea. "It's not your fault. You're a chick. Chicks can't paint. Painting is for men. Chicks should do other things. Pretty things. What about poetry? That's a nice thing for a chick to do, in her spare time." Rick kissed me, then picked up a rag, soaked it in turpentine, and cleaned the paint off my arm.

I quit painting and wrote poetry. Rick hated my poetry. I went over to his house a few weeks later and listened to him tell me why.

"It needs more of this, Ellen," Rick said, opening his desk drawer, taking out a gun, and waving it around like a drunken cowboy. My poems were in front of him on the desk. Rick hammered them with the gun butt. "It needs more of *this*." BAM! "It needs more of *this*." BAM!

When I told Susie the story, she was horrified. It didn't seem as strange to me as it did to her. All the boys I knew had guns, in Montana. Rick had been surprised too, when I wasn't scared.

I stopped writing poetry and became a literature major. Rick thought this was a good idea. If I didn't get married, I could always teach.

Rick never talked about himself or his family. Everything I knew about him came from others. People were only too happy to tell me all they knew, or imagined. I heard Rick was brilliant, but weird. That he did psychology experiments on all his girlfriends. By the time he dropped them, he had them drooling, like Pavlov's dog. He had them sitting up, rolling over, playing dead, and begging. I heard he was bisexual and having an affair with my French professor, Monsieur Beausoleil, a vindictive little shit who would surely fail me if he found out I was seeing Rick, so I had better keep a low profile. Monsieur Beausoleil wore scarves. He gave one to Rick every time they balled, or so I heard.

I heard Rick was the son of the head of the Jewish Mafia. (That was where all the money came from.) He paid his tuition in cash, in hundred-dollar bills, a girl who worked in the registrar's office told me. Some psych majors filled me in on his rat lab experiments, which Rick planned to apply to people when he joined the family business. By then, he'd know which was the most addictive: cocaine, sex, or heroin. I heard I had better watch out.

A girl in my French class had slept with Rick for a

while, she told me without being asked, after she saw us together. Eliza Perry, a statuesque Texan, had slept with Rick and the musician Charles Lloyd at the same time, or so she claimed. Charles Lloyd came to Portland at least once a year—to trade in stale members of his entourage for young, fresh faces—just like the Living Theater did. They treated Reed like a giant used car lot, or fish pond. Eliza had been thrown back six months ago. Now she was sleeping with Ken Cobb, an American Literature professor, who probably wouldn't have bothered with her if she hadn't been Charles Lloyd's ex-girlfriend. Eliza, who had once had a rock band called Eliza and the Vipers, who had worn black leather head to toe and carried a whip, told me Rick scared her. I asked her why.

"The first night I made love to him," she said in her breathy little-girl voice, "I dreamed my breasts had been removed by a skillful surgeon."

"Far out," I said dryly. Eliza nodded. Under Charles Lloyd's influence, Eliza had gone spiritual. She had joined Wicca. She wore shawls and carried Tarot cards in her purse. She was a fruitarian. She only ate what the earth gave up *voluntarily*, like nuts, ripe apples, and drugs. Anything else was murder one. This was a hard line to follow in Oregon in the winter. Eliza admitted she couldn't hack it. While she lectured me about Rick, she chain-smoked Winstons, filled with dead tobacco. I didn't put a whole lot of credence in what she said, though her parting shot worried me.

She said, "Rick has another girlfriend."

"So what?" I said, trying to control my voice. Jealousy was so *uncool*.

"A *serious* girlfriend. Anna Watson. She's my best friend. She's doing her junior year abroad, in Paris. At the Sorbonne. She's a genius," Eliza said proudly.

I yawned. Most of us were geniuses, more or less. "So what else is new?"

"Oh, nothing special. Only when she gets back, *you're*

*gonna be up shit creek,''* Eliza said, in a phony deep-South accent. Anna Watson couldn't be all that smart. No real genius would have Eliza for a best friend.

Eliza lit up another Winston. She was a regular tobacco crematorium. I reached over and stroked her orange suede boots. "Oooooh, what are these made of? Dead cow?" I said.

That night, I asked Rick about the stories I'd heard. He said all the stories were true, then told me about his rat lab experiments. The rats liked cocaine better than sex or heroin. They'd push the lever for coke instead of food every time. They'd do it until they starved to death, Rick said.

Rick got a tiny vial out of his desk and offered me some coke. I said no. I said I had an eight o'clock.

"Some other time," I said. My voice was cold, but my hands were shaking. Rick shook his head, smiling slightly, like I had surprised him. *Exasperated* him. He put the coke away. I didn't ask him about Anna Watson.

A week after Thanksgiving, I found out Rick had been sleeping with Susie. Juanita Kazin, who aspired to being a sex therapist, told me. I wanted to smash her face in. Everybody on campus probably knew about it but me.

I asked Rick about it first. He didn't seem to give a shit.

"I went over there one day and she was there and you weren't," Rick said casually, looking bored. "She was a nice fuck, so I came back for more, once or twice." I started to cry. "We're not *engaged*, Ellen," Rick said. "We're not *going steady*. Don't make such a big deal out of it. It was nothing. Less than nothing. I like you better anyway. Susie's a moron. If you'd been home when you should've been, it never would've happened." I walked back to Foster in a trance. Rick liked me. *Liked* me. I *loved* him.

"I'm sorry," Susie said, when she came in and saw

me packing my meager possessions. She didn't bother to ask why I was packing. I had Joni Mitchell on the stereo. I was just about all cried out.

"You're not sorry at all," I said coldly. "You're just sorry you got caught."

"I didn't think you'd care," Susie said. I had one boyfriend. Susie had dozens. I couldn't believe she'd be such a lousy friend.

"You *knew* I'd care. You went ahead and did it anyway."

"It was just sex. It didn't *mean* anything."

"Not to you. It means something to me."

Susie started to cry. "We didn't tell you because we didn't want to hurt you."

"What goes around comes around, Susie," I said.

I didn't move out that night, but the next day I went to the housing office. Luckily there were lots of dropouts. People dropped out of Reed every year in droves. They couldn't do the work, which was immense and difficult, without the discipline they probably got at home, in high school, from their teachers and parents. They couldn't hack it without somebody constantly on their backs, the weaklings, the wimps. No, not everybody could have an active sex life, take large quantities of drugs, and still keep up with their schoolwork like I could, aided and abetted by speed, of course. (Every year the school doctor, Dr. Lipshitz, went to the Faculty Senate and said he was prescribing far too many drugs. He said too many students were asking for speed, to stay awake, so we could do our work, and for Valium, so we could come down off the speed and sleep, every third night or so. He recounted the relevant statistics. He told the faculty they were working us too hard. The faculty thanked him politely for coming, then replied that work wasn't the problem, *we* were the problem. We failed to use our time productively. Dr. Lipshitz sighed and went back to the infirmary, to write a few dozen more prescriptions. At least if we got it from him, it would be uncut.)

I got a room in the old dorm block with a fireplace and a somewhat bigger bed. My roommate, Selma Rabinowitz, was in love with a Black Panther from Oakland who beat her regularly. Selma spent a lot of time in the infirmary. She was hardly ever around. I got back together with Rick, but he never said he loved me. I never said it either. The boy had to say it first. I don't think Rick ever tried to sleep with Selma, but he might have. If he didn't, it was only because Curtis Haywood was so big and mean.

Susie barely made it through the semester. Without me there to help her, the quality of her schoolwork plunged dramatically. I heard she'd applied for a transfer to USC, which was just about her speed, I thought coldly, hating her. She shouldn't have come to Reed in the first place. When we passed each other in the halls, we didn't speak.

I went back to Montana for Christmas. We had all of January off, to enrich ourselves culturally, so my mother got me a job clerking at the North Side Superette, which my Uncle Ralph manages. I filled in for Margie Smith, who was taking a month off to have another baby. I was lucky to get the job. With the money I made from it, I would be able to buy my own books. I would have to, now that Susie and I weren't friends.

During January, I wrote Rick, who was home in Miami, every other day. Rick didn't write me at all, though he called once a week. When school started in February, Susie wasn't there. I never saw her again.

Ken Cobb was the coolest person on campus. He had gone to Harvard with Timothy Leary. He had lived in Millbrook with Leary and Alan Watts. He was radical, mystical, bisexual. He took enormous amounts of drugs. Before this was all common knowledge, Cobb had gotten tenure. Now he could do anything he wanted and never be fired.

Cobb's little house in Westmoreland was a home away from home for those of us who wanted to be cool or were cool already. I felt privileged to be there, though I hardly ever opened my mouth. I was the only freshman in American Literature 401, which met Wednesday nights at Cobb's. I wasn't sure how I had gotten in, but suspected it was because of Rick. He and Cobb were old friends.

Every Wednesday night, Rick came to pick me up after class. Sometimes he stayed and had a drink with Cobb. They drank Scotch together. The rest of us drank cheap red wine. Cobb stood too close to Rick and talked to him exclusively, cutting everybody else out. If Cobb got *far* too close, Rick put his hand on Cobb's chest and pushed him away. But if the class was still going on when Rick arrived, and he wanted to leave, we left. Rick didn't mind interrupting the class. He would walk in the front door without knocking, find me, stand in front of the low red-velvet couch I favored, stick out his hands, and pull me to my feet.

"Get your coat, Ellen," Rick would say, cutting off whoever happened to be talking.

"You look like you're *hypnotized*," Jade O'Malley, a Korean war orphan from Sayville, Long Island, said to me one night. "Is he, really, you know, like *good*, or something?"

Was he? I didn't know. He was better than most boys in the getting-it-up department. He always had it up. He was always ready. We did it hard and for a long time. Rick would move me into these different positions. I guess he was good. But he never talked sweetly to me. He was never affectionate. He hardly ever kissed me. After we did it, Rick studied. There were two down quilts on his bed, one for him and one for me. Except when we were actually doing it, he really didn't like to touch me. He didn't like me touching him. When he finished studying, he'd turn off the lights without asking if I was ready to go to sleep.

One night, when Rick was late and Cobb was holding court downstairs, I climbed the ladder to Cobb's bedroom with a book, a glass of wine, and a hit of speed. I had never been in Cobb's bedroom before. The bed was inside an iron cage, like a cell. The cage door was open. There was a white fur rug on the floor. I was reading *Pilgrim's Progress* when Cobb came up the ladder. He sat down on the bed and rubbed my back.

"I guess I should go," I said.

Cobb said, "You don't have to."

"Okay, I won't."

"You should forget about Rick Lansky," Cobb said, taking off his purple wire rims and massaging the bridge of his nose. Cobb looked old and tired. His ponytail was shot with gray. "He'll hurt you. You're too nice for him."

I was insulted. Nice! Nice wasn't dangerous, or sexy, or glamorous. My newest heroine, Anita Pallenberg, Keith Richards' old lady and the star of *Performance*, which Rick and I had seen something like eight or nine times, wasn't *nice*. "I'm not nice at all," I said. Rick hated nice.

"Oh, yes, you are," said Cobb. "You're a very nice girl, Ellen. You should quit pretending that you aren't a nice girl and go back home, find a nice boy to love you, and get married." Married! Who did he think I was?

"I'm not like that at all," I said coldly. "You've got the wrong idea about me."

Cobb shook his head. I heard footsteps on the porch. Cobb put on his glasses and went downstairs. I rolled over, sat up straight, whipped out my compact, and put on lipstick. Then I lay back down on my stomach and pretended to read. A few minutes later I heard footsteps on the ladder. I didn't look up.

"Fetching," Rick said, sitting down on the bed. I had

on a denim midi-skirt and red platform boots. Rick put his hand up my skirt but he didn't turn me over. "Quite fetching."

"Not there," I said, when I realized what he was up to.

"Why not there?"

"It hurts." I didn't know for a fact that it actually *did* hurt, but it seemed reasonable to me that it probably *would* hurt. "I don't like pain," I said. I put down *Pilgrim's Progress*, knocked his hand away, and rolled over.

"Oh, I think maybe you do," Rick said. "I think you just don't know yourself very well."

I shrugged. "Whatever," I said, with a rare show of independence. I took off my blouse slowly, provocatively. Rick smiled. He seemed pleased at the change in me. He liked girls who were strong, but not *too* strong. He took off his pants. We did it my way.

In April, we went on strike. The issues were these: tenure for two fired Marxist professors, student representation on the Faculty Senate, no more required courses, and ending the Vietnam War.

I was galvanized by the strike. I loved making signs and building barricades. It satisfied my thwarted desire for painting and sculpture. The strike was run by the boys, of course, but there were plenty of things for us girls to do, like making coffee, going for sandwiches, and fucking.

Rick hated the strike and the strikers. He thought it was a good idea to bomb the Communists back to the Stone Age. He idolized General Westmoreland and Barry Goldwater. He thought there weren't *enough* required courses. Worst of all, the rat lab was in Eliot Hall, which we were occupying. Rick couldn't get in to run his rats, though the Strike Committee had promised the rats would be well treated. We almost broke up again, because of the strike, but we didn't. We compromised.

Every other night, after it got dark, I would crawl out a bathroom window in Eliot Hall and go to Rick, who was waiting for me in his Mercedes in front of the library. Rick would take me downtown for an expensive dinner. We would go to his house and fuck. At dawn, I would get up, walk back to Eliot Hall, and crawl in the bathroom window.

One night, Rick took me to Jake's for seafood. The specialty was soft-shell crabs, which I had never eaten. Rick ordered some for me. The crabs were so tiny. I was living on peanut butter and crackers. It was hard to get the meat out of those little shells. Pretty soon my plate was a mess. I had eaten about two bites. I looked up and noticed Rick, laughing with his mouth closed. I had no idea why he was laughing. He was laughing so hard he was almost crying from the strain of keeping the laughter in. Rick hated people who laughed out loud. He hated scenes, too, and I was about to make one. I started to cry.

"Ellen . . ." he said gently. "Don't cry. I'm sorry. It was a bad joke." Rick picked up my knife and fork. He cut off a claw and fed it to me whole.

"Good?" he said. I nodded. It was crispy and delicious. I wiped my eyes and ate the crabs.

The following week, I sneaked out the bathroom window and went to a fish market in Chinatown and bought half a dozen soft-shell crabs. It was Rick's twentieth birthday. I wanted to make him dinner.

Rick came into the kitchen and watched me cook. I picked up each little crab, dipped it in egg batter, then in flour and almonds. I heated the oil and dropped the crabs into the pan. They tried to crawl out. I slammed a lid on the pan. Rick was laughing silently.

"Oh, Ellen . . ." he said. The pan rocked back and forth on the stove, like a van full of people fucking. Rick held down the lid with both hands.

"I didn't know they were still alive! How could I? I'm from Montana," I said miserably.

"It wasn't your fault."

"They were so *still*."

"They should have cleaned them for you, at the fish market. They're probably dead by now." The pan had stopped moving. Rick took the lid off, peeked in, and nodded. "Yep. All dead."

"I couldn't eat them now," I said. "But I will if you want to." Rick turned off the stove, took me downtown, and taught me how to eat lobster.

The strike ended without anything being resolved. Summer came. Everybody went home. Rick Lansky was the big loser in the '71 strike. When the kids occupying Eliot Hall had gone, Rick found out the rat lab was empty. Someone had liberated the lab rats! They would have a tough time feeding their little habits outside, except for the ones who were addicted to sex.

Rick had to stay in Portland for the summer, to redo his experiment with a fresh group of rats. I decided to stay in Portland too. I hoped Rick would ask me to live with him, but he didn't.

I got a job as a proofreader at the *Oregonian* and moved into a house near the river, across the street from the Pancake House, with Selma Rabinowitz and four other girls. Tuition was going up in the fall, but my scholarship wasn't. I had to save every penny. When Rick didn't feed me, I lived on rice and beans.

During the summer, we went to the races. Rick bet carefully. Usually, he won. I bet the money he gave me on horses with names I liked: Joltin' Joe, Lambchop, Heavy Karma. I lost the money immediately.

One day, when we were on our way to the races, Rick said, "Don't you have anything else to wear?" I only had one outfit Rick liked, the denim suit, and it was too hot for denim. I shook my head. I knew Rick hated my clothes. "It makes you look like a hippie," he had said one night, with distaste, of the paisley maxi-dress I had on. He hated my flannel shirts and Redwing hiking boots. He hated long skirts, antique jackets, op-art prints, bell-bottoms, velvet, embroidery, and fringe on anything. "I thought I was *supposed* to look like a hippie," I had said.

"And your underwear," Rick went on, sticking his hand up under my skirt and fingering a piece of frayed elastic as if it were the tail of a dead rat. My underwear, bought by my mother two years ago from the Montgomery Ward catalog, was disgraceful. I knew that. "Not very erotic, Ellen. Don't you have anything different?"

"I don't have anything different because I don't have any money," I said, choking back tears. "I don't have any money at all. My parents don't have any money. There isn't any money for underwear."

"You should have told me," Rick said, like he was really surprised. He probably thought I was middle class, a small-town doctor's daughter or something. Anything else was beyond belief. He probably thought I was slumming.

Rick took me downtown and bought me a summer wardrobe. He bought me shorts and gauzy cotton slacks and French-cut T-shirts and silk blouses and Italian sandals. He bought me three bathing suits, even though I couldn't swim. He bought me open-toed heels, clunky platforms, and black lace underwear. I hadn't worn a bra, not for two years. I hadn't shaved my legs or underarms either. Before Rick took me downtown shopping, he made me go into the bathroom and shave. He bought me two identical linen suits, one white and one black.

After we went shopping, Rick took me to the Benson for brunch. We ate sparingly, drank lots of champagne, then checked into a suite for the day. Rick dressed me and then undressed me, over and over. Then he took me down to the hotel beauty shop and had them cut my hair like Anita Pallenberg's. I walked out of the Benson with my hair cut to my jawline and long heavy bangs, in a black linen suit, stockings, and four-inch heels. When we got back to Rick's house, he made me take off the white silk blouse I had on under the suit, opened his bulging scarf drawer, and picked out a red and black scarf that Monsieur Beausoleil used to wear to French class. Rick draped it around my neck, put the jacket back on me, and tucked the scarf under the lapels.

I went to Kalispell late in August to see my parents. Rick went to Miami. He didn't write or phone. I thought about calling collect, but I was ashamed to.

When I got back to Portland, I didn't call Rick. I didn't want to seem too eager. I would see him on Wednesday night where I always saw him, at Cobb's. That semester we were studying the American Transcendentalists. I wore the black linen suit Rick had bought me though it was too cold for linen. Cobb told me I looked lovely, but everybody else stared. They thought I was weird. Nobody wore suits to school, not even teachers.

Rick didn't come. The class ended. I went upstairs to Cobb's bed and cried. Cobb rubbed my back and gave me a double Scotch. He asked me if I wanted to stay, but I didn't.

I walked over to Rick's house. The front door was unlocked. I heard sounds coming from the bedroom, tiptoed to the door, and put my ear up against it. I heard a woman's voice, then Rick's. He was *laughing*, out *loud*. Rick and the woman laughed and laughed. I walked home in a trance. I was always doing that in Portland, walking home in trances, in the rain, without an umbrella. I couldn't stop crying. Anna Watson had come home.

I saw them together the next day, in front of the library where I worked. They had their arms around each other. They were practically fucking on the steps. When I walked by, head down, trying not to watch, Rick didn't even notice.

Later I saw Anna on the lawn. She was arm in arm with Eliza Perry. I could see why Anna and Eliza were best friends. They were like Susie and I had been: Snow White and Rose Red, only taller, prettier. Anna was really exotic, with beautifully tanned skin (maybe she had been in Miami with Rick) and long black frizzy hair framing a strange, dramatic face, like Queen Nefertiti. I felt totally outclassed. When they passed me, Eliza whispered something in Anna's ear and laughed. Anna turned and stared. I stared back. Anna smiled. It wasn't a mean smile. I tried to smile too, but I wasn't quite able to. I wasn't ready to smile at Anna Watson just yet. I couldn't pull it off. Anna walked away like a dancer, with her feet pointed out. She wore pink ballet shoes, a T-shirt, jeans, a black leather jacket, and one of Monsieur Beausoleil's scarves.

After that, I didn't see Rick at all. I saw quite a few other boys—mathematicians, physicists, philosophy majors, a violinist—and manipulated them, the way Rick had manipulated me. I ran them ragged. I had them begging for mercy. After Rick, every other boy was child's play. I found out I had power too. I can't say I didn't use it.

I discovered Lower Commons, where the pool tables and pinball machines were. Sometimes I watched *Star Trek* reruns. Lower Commons was a good place to meet boys, nice boys, the kind who didn't give me much trouble.

One night, Anna Watson wandered into Lower Commons alone. I was playing pinball. Anna came over to watch.

"Do you want to play?" I said. Anna didn't speak or put down any quarters. Her pretty brown eyes were glazed. I played another game, but I didn't do well. I hate to be watched when I'm playing pinball. The balls slid down the gutters. I was getting the creeps from Anna, who was swaying back and forth like a snake. I finished the game, picked up my bag, and walked away. Anna followed. I leaned against the pool table and waited for her to catch up. Anna stood in front of me, her shins pressed against my knees.

"Do you know what an oxymoron is?" she said. Some genius! "Look what he gave me." Anna held out a leaf, with OXYMORON printed on it in red Crayola. She kept trying to get closer to me, like she was cold and I was the furnace.

"Oxymoron," Anna read. Her breath had a metallic scent. When I leaned backward, away from her, Anna leaned in. I noticed her left hand all of a sudden, the one holding the leaf. She was missing the first joints of her fingers.

"It's a figure of speech," I said.

"It sounds ugly, like a stupid cow."

"That's not what it is at all. It's a contradiction in terms. The deafening silence. The lonely crowd." Anna looked at me blankly. "Who gave it to you? Rick?" Anna nodded, eyes wide, like I was a friend of hers or something. She didn't even *know* me. She'd forgotten I was Rick's other girlfriend. She didn't even know who I was. "If he called you an oxymoron, it probably means he finds you fascinating," I said dryly. "I couldn't say why." I straightened up and pushed Anna away. I pushed her harder than I meant to, or so I told myself later, when I was feeling really guilty about it. Anna lost her balance and dropped her leaf. I stepped on it.

"I'm sorry," I muttered, then turned on my heel and fled. At the door, I looked back. Anna just stood there, twirling the crushed leaf. I couldn't just leave her standing there alone. I was a nice girl, after all. I *used* to be. I went back.

"Anna, are you okay?" I said. Anna didn't speak. Tears were streaming down her face. Rick Lansky had that effect on girls. I took her by the arm and led her to the couch. We sat down. I put my arms around her. I listened to her babble on and on, about what a shit Rick was and how she'd dumped another boy in Paris for him, a *nice* boy, one with a *title*, and he had loved her but

Rick didn't love her at all and she didn't even *like* him but tonight he was with someone else, a freshman, she had *seen* them together, and it was killing her.

"Why do I put *up* with it?" she kept saying, over and over and over. After a while it got boring. I'd heard it all before, inside my own head. Anna's voice got weaker and weaker. Her words were slurred, nonsensical. She wound down finally. I got up to play more pinball. Anna toppled over on the couch.

When I got back a half hour later, Anna was dead to the world. I thought about calling Rick to pick her up, like the laundry, but I didn't. Anna would hate me for it. I decided to take her home myself.

I couldn't wake Anna up. She was out cold. Worse, her breathing was raspy. Her mouth was open, loose. She *drooled*. I splashed a handful of water on her face. No response. I started to get scared, to put it all together: the glazed eyes, the slurring, the deep dark sleep. Anna Watson couldn't hold her drugs. I looked around for help, but there wasn't any. The pay phone in Lower Commons was broken. I rolled Anna over onto her back and put a pillow under her neck, so she wouldn't choke. The infirmary was a hundred yards away. I ran.

Two days later, I went to see Anna in the hospital. She'd had her stomach pumped. Her parents thanked me over and over.

"She's never been the same, since the motorcycle accident," Mrs. Watson said more than once. Anna had been a concert pianist. "I don't understand her. Do *you* understand her, Ellen?"

"No. Not really," I said.

Eliza Perry thanked me too. She gave me a deck of Tarot cards, a copy of *The Teachings of Don Juan*, and a kiss. But Anna didn't thank me. She didn't even want to see me. When I went into her room, she wouldn't speak. She turned her back. When I picked up her mangled hand and squeezed it, Anna pulled it away.

Anna's parents took her out of school and back to Chicago. The following Wednesday, Rick showed up at Cobb's. I was ready for him.

He said, "Get your coat, Ellen." He stood in front of me and held out his hands, but I didn't take them. My own hands were shaking. I sat on them.

"I've got other plans," I said.

Rick couldn't believe it. He kept standing there with his hands out while somebody droned on about *Blithedale Romance* and I looked right through him, until Cobb said, "Would you like to sit down and join the class, Richard?" Rick cursed and stalked out.

During the next month, Rick chased me. He sent flowers, candy, jewelry, the works. He sent a black leather jacket that looked suspiciously like Anna's, but this one was new. It still had its tags. I held out for a while, then let Rick take me home and fuck me for a long time—this way, that way, any way he wanted. Rick was lying back and smoking a Gauloise, all relaxed and happy and pleased with himself, sated, when I sprung my little surprise.

"Take me home now," I said coldly. "That was goodbye."

*"What?"*

I got up and started putting on the clothes Rick bought me, the red high heels, the black lace panties. "Take me home. It's over."

"A *mercy* fuck?" he said.

"Whatever. You don't love me and I don't love you. It's just sex. I want something better."

Rick smiled broadly. "You deserve it, Ellen."

Before we left, Rick made me a Scotch and soda. We had a goodbye toast, for old times' sake. We sat around and rapped, just like we were friends. But Rick's eyes weren't friendly at all. He was really mad. He scared me.

In the car, he said, "It's funny, after all this time. *You* walking out on *me*."

"Some fun," I said. "I figured it was time. I don't want to end up like Anna Watson."

"That Anna," Rick said fondly.

"Who was driving that motorcycle anyway? You?"

Rick laughed. "Does it matter?" Then: "Did you know? Anna has two vaginas."

"Nobody has two vaginas."

"Anna does." Rick reached over and touched me under my denim skirt. "There . . . and there."

"So that was why you dumped me, huh?" I said, taking his hand away.

"Uh huh. A chance like that only comes along once in a lifetime."

"I guess I don't feel so bad about it then."

"You shouldn't," Rick said.

When we got to my house, Rick kissed me. He said, "You're doing the right thing, Ellen. I don't blame you a bit." Then: "We're pretty well matched, don't you think? You and me?"

"Not anymore. We were once. But when we were, you didn't notice."

"You never loved me, did you?"

"You never loved *me*."

"That's different," Rick said.

"Is it? If you want to know the truth, you're right: I never loved you," I lied. "Not ever. I was just testing my wings. See you around." I went into the house and double-locked the door. Rick wouldn't let it go like this. I was sure of it. He *hated* to lose. My heart was pounding. Everything was pulsing ominously. Maybe Rick had drugged me. That was it! The farewell drink! *Rick had put acid in my Scotch.* I started hallucinating, just a tiny bit, right around the edges of my eyes.

There was a boy in my living room building a fire in the fireplace: Denny Kirshner, a senior from Palo Alto. I recognized him from school. He was the Oregon chairman of Youth for McGovern. He was always trying to register people to vote, a thankless task. He was dating

Barbara Boynton, one of my roommates, but Barbara
wasn't there yet. She was at the Women's Center, probably, where she often said I should be, getting her
consciousness raised.

Denny Kirshner was redheaded, freckle-faced, clean-
cut. He looked like Opie on *Andy Griffith*, Howdy
Doody come to life. He was the kind of guy who wanted
to make changes *within the system*. Poor Denny. Totally fucking boring. But I was alone. There was nobody else there.

I told Denny Kirshner all about Rick Lansky. I told
him Rick had undoubtedly drugged me and that I was
flipping out. Denny took me into the kitchen and made
me a vodka and orange juice.

"O.J. is good for bad trips," Denny said. "All that
Vitamin C." He rummaged around in the medicine cabinet and found some Valium. I ate four. Denny took the
bottle away from me, pocketed it. He held my hands
while I babbled on and on, then stood behind my chair
and rubbed my neck. I chugged the drink. Denny made
me another. By the time I realized I wasn't tripping, I
was drunk.

"Aren't you supposed to be Barbara's boyfriend?" I
said as Denny carried me upstairs. Barbara was supposed
to be my friend.

"Not if you don't want me to be," Denny said. He
was awfully strong, for a liberal. "We don't have to make
love," he said, as he lowered me to the bed.

"Don't you want to?" I asked.

"Of course I want to."

"Why wait for anything, when you can have it right
now?"

"Oh, my," said Denny. "You're quite a handful, aren't
you?" I guess I was at that. I didn't used to be quite a
handful. I used to be a very nice girl.

"You know where the door is," I said, pointing to it.
"Take your innocence and run!"

Denny laughed, stayed. We made love. It was strange.

"Do you like this?" Denny asked. "What about that? Does it feel good?" he kept saying. He kept *asking me how I felt*. I wasn't used to it. It was interesting, I guess. It seemed healthy, sort of. I might've had an orgasm. I think I did.

Barbara freaked out when she got home and found us. I got the blame, of course. Denny kissed me goodbye and fled. All the other girls in the house sided with Barbara, even Selma. They caucused in the kitchen, then asked me to move out.

"I was drunk," I said. They caucused again, then came back with the verdict: Being Drunk Is No Excuse.

"How could you be such a rotten friend?" Barbara kept saying. "How could you be such a lousy sister?" I hung my head and cried.

"I'm sorry," I said over and over, but I wasn't sorry at all. I was sorry I'd gotten caught.

I packed and moved in with Denny, who had a whole house to himself, just like Rick did. (It was so much cheaper that way, both of them explained, in almost the same words: to buy instead of rent.) Then I reboxed the leather jacket Rick sent me, took it downtown to the store it came from and traded it for three hundred dollars' worth of art supplies.

That summer, Denny took me to San Francisco, to a Youth for McGovern convention. We stayed in a hotel near Fisherman's Wharf. At a fund-raising dinner, we sat with Leonard Nimoy. I wore my white linen suit and one of Mrs. Kirshner's fur boas. Denny's parents were ex-Communists. They didn't mind the fact that I was poor. Why, Mr. Kirshner had once been poor himself! If I wanted to go to the San Francisco Art Institute while Denny was at Stanford Law, the Kirshners would pay my way.

George McGovern's campaign manager sat on my right. He was cute, but married. Despite or because of this, he gave me the once-over. So did Leonard Nimoy.

"I've heard about you Reed girls," Leonard Nimoy said. I didn't ask him what he'd heard. I didn't care. Leonard Nimoy's eyes slanted down instead of up. He looked like an alien, without his ears. Under the white tablecloth, I put my hand in Denny's lap and squeezed. Denny blushed.

After dinner, I took Denny to a midnight screening of *Performance*, my favorite movie. He hated it.

"Nobody ever goes outside," he said accusingly, as we walked out of the theater. Denny loved outside. He was always dragging *me* there.

"Of *course* they go outside," I said.

"Only once, after they all get in the house. Then they only go as far as the greenhouse. To get drugs," he said.

The next day, while Denny was out saving the world, I went shopping with Denny's money. Late in the day, hands full of packages, I saw Gail Lindstrom panhandling in the Haight. She looked straight at me. I told her my name, but she didn't know me. Her pupils were as big as plates. I gave her one of Denny's twenties. She didn't thank me. She didn't even close her palm around the bill. It blew out of her hand. I stepped on the twenty, picked it up, and tucked it in a pocket of her filthy jacket, the same once-white, fringed and beaded jacket she'd worn to run away with the Electric Flag. All the beads were gone, I noticed. When I walked away, Gail had a piece of the fringe in her mouth. She chewed it placidly, like a cow, until it slipped out. Then she picked up another piece and chewed on that. Every piece of fringe on the front of Gail's jacket had been nibbled. The leather was stained with bloody saliva. Gail had lost a number of teeth.

I went back to the hotel and called my mother in Kalispell, at the North Side Superette, where she was filling in for Margie Smith, who was having her tubes tied. I told my mother about Gail. We cried, but we didn't call the Lindstroms. We didn't want to interfere. Our families had never been all that close. Gail Lindstrom had never been my friend.

# Song of the Fucked Duck

Marissa Van Horn was late. She decided to take the shortcut to Milly Averitt's, where she was expected for cocktails. It was muddy on the path, so Marissa put on her Nikes, carried her heels, and gathered up her skirt in front of her. She was jogging down the path that circled the lake, connecting Milly's property to hers, when she stumbled across two Haggerty boys, raping a duck: pants around ankles, pencil-thin staffs at attention, terrified squawking duck, smell of blood and duck shit made it all too clear. Everyone froze except the duck, which continued to flap its wings pitifully.

Marissa's heels were pink satin, dyed to match her dress. She raised one of them over her head. "You! Abner Haggerty! Let that duck be!"

The Haggerty in question wiped his nose with the back of his hand. "My duck, I caught it," he said. Then, under his breath: "You old witch."

"My *lake*," said Marissa, waving the shoe. Abner rammed into the duck one last time, then yanked it off him with a wet sucking pop. The duck squealed and fell to the ground. The Haggertys backed into the woods, screaming every bad word they knew. Marissa picked up the duck, wrapped it in her pink chiffon skirt, set her heels down beside it, and walked back the way she came.

* * *

"Isn't there a law in this country against bestiality?" Marissa asked Doc Dixon an hour later.

" 'Gainst what, Rissy?" The doctor was stitching up the duck's torn rectum.

"*You* know what," Marissa said.

"I expect so. Crime against nature and all that. Expect it never gets enforced, round these parts. People bein' people. He'll be fine, Rissy." The doctor patted the duck on the head. "Leave it be."

"On my *lake*," she said, for the second time that night. "I don't like things like that happening, on my lake."

The doctor eyed Marissa skeptically, not liking what he saw: the beady blue eyes too close together, the sharp sallow face, the nonexistent chin. Rissy Van Horn always had been stubborn, he thought. Too stubborn for her own damned good.

Marissa took the duck home and made him a bed out of old cotillion dresses. The duck quacked feebly, then slept. The bloody pink chiffon went into the trash.

In the morning, Marissa called the SPCA. They told her she could file charges against the Haggertys if she wanted to. Marissa did, and her word meant something. It wasn't called Van Horn County for nothing, not that it ever did Rissy much good, man-wise. The boys were tried and sentenced. The Haggertys cursed and shook their fists. The whole town was embarrassed for Marissa, for making such a fuss out of nothing, since boys will be boys and so on. Marissa stopped going out for cocktails, or to the club. She spent more and more time with the duck.

When the duck was almost well, Marissa took him to the lake. She put on her swimsuit and carried him in, feeling like Brother Boone, about to do a baptism. But when Marissa took her arms out from under the duck, he shivered and sank like a stone. Marissa lifted him up and tried again. The duck looked at her hard and sank. Marissa fished him out and carried him back to the house. In the six-person claw-footed bathtub her daddy had bought

bought from a New Orleans brothel, or so the story went—but Marissa had never believed it—the duck swam happily. Marissa sat by the tub and watched. In her mind, she saw a picture of the duck the night he was raped. He was swimming along all peaceful-like, happy to be alive, when Abner Haggerty, lurking in the reeds, *breathing* through one of them, grabbed his little orange feet and pulled him under. Marissa didn't know *why* she knew how it happened, but she did.

Marissa put the duck in her own bed that night, after he was clean, and stroked him gently.

"I love you, duck," Marissa said. She kissed the top of his little white head impulsively, then got up to turn out the bathroom light.

When Marissa came back, the duck was gone. A man was there instead. He looked like Superman only better, Marissa thought. She couldn't get over it: a naked man on a pile of feathers. Marissa rubbed her eyes, waiting for him to disappear. When he didn't, she stepped out of her nightgown and into bed. She had always believed in fairy tales.

It was a good thing Marissa picked that night to kiss the duck, since a couple of the older Haggertys had already cut her phone line and were eager to do to Marissa what they'd already done to their *own* ducks, not to mention their sheep, chickens, baby calves, and sluggish sisters. The very thing some big boys in the reform school had done to their two little brothers, or so they'd heard. Over and over and *over*.

After Marissa's lights went out, the Haggertys closed in. Their bodies were never found. The duck and Marissa lived happily ever after, though everybody wondered where he'd come from so quiet-like, and what a man as good-looking as Mr. R. N. Drake saw in a scrawny old maid like Rissy.

# Mr. and Mrs. Skeritt

During the eleventh year of their marriage, Mrs. Skeritt's husband George began to change.

The change began from the bottom up, with his feet.
Mrs. Skeritt urged him to see a podiatrist, but George
didn't hold much with doctors. He spent half a week's
salary at Modern Drugs, trying to cure himself. He
bought Out-Gro and Penetro and Cornhuskers Lotion and
nearly everything on the Dr. Bronner's rack and insoles
for the fishing boots he could still get his feet into comfortably, but none of it helped George at all.

When he got tired of the boys at the Texaco razzing
him for wearing those rubber boots every day, George
stopped going to work entirely. Soon he never even left
the house, not to go to the Golden Frog Pool Hall, where
it was always 68 degrees inside, or to Chester's Bar and
Grill, or even to Jakey Stallcup's for Friday-night poker.
Mrs. Skeritt had never known George to miss a Friday
at Jakey's, even when Friday fell on Christmas. But
George was changing. He wouldn't speak to his buddies
when they called him on the phone. Soon the calls
stopped coming. This made George angry.

"Nobody appreciates George Skeritt anymore," he
snarled to his wife, when she came in to feed him. "I'll
show 'em! See if I don't. Sonsabitches'll get theirs."

George always was a tad melodramatic, Mrs. Skeritt

119

thought, emptying an ashtray. And here he was again, making a fuss out of nothing. They'd stopped asking after him at church too. George never was what you'd call popular. But when George refused to go downtown to the Welfare to apply for disability or even food stamps, Mrs. Skeritt got worried.

"If anyone deserves it, God knows, George honey—" she would begin hopefully, but George snarled impatiently and cut her off every time. George didn't want to be beholden to no one, especially not to the Federal Government, which he hated bitterly, though his beloved Republicans were in power again at last. The government was overrun with Communists, George said. Had been ever since that Jew bastard Roosevelt. It would take a good long time to run 'em all out. Mrs. Skeritt might have been talking to a wall. Their small savings dwindled rapidly.

Mrs. Skeritt took a waitressing job on Jacksboro Highway, so her two kids, Danny and Lynda, wouldn't starve. Waitressing was the only job Mrs. Skeritt could get, and she was lucky to find that. Mrs. Skeritt had never worked outside the home. George said it wouldn't be fittin'.

Mrs. Skeritt took the bus to work every day, and the first few days were hard ones. Almost no one in Fort Worth rode the bus. There was no one to talk to and nothing to look at. It was a long, slow ride. Mrs. Skeritt had never learned to drive. George had never let her.

One day in the checkout line at Piggly Wiggly, Mrs. Skeritt picked up a paperback book. She didn't look at the title, just grabbed it off the rack and bought it quick, before she could change her mind. It was a Louis L'Amour western. For the next few days on the bus, Mrs. Skeritt read that. *Hondo* didn't impress her much, but Mrs. Skeritt enjoyed the reading of it. When she was a girl, Mrs. Skeritt loved to read. She hadn't had time to, since her marriage to George.

When she finished *Hondo*, Mrs. Skeritt got worried. Books were expensive. She couldn't just buy another one when her kids weren't eating right. One of the girls at work made a suggestion, and the following Saturday Mrs. Skeritt and the kids went downtown. BRING YOUR PROBLEMS TO THE LIBRARY a banner across the entrance proclaimed. It was National Library Week. All three of them got cards. Mrs. Skeritt couldn't believe how easy it was.

On the bus trip home, nobody spoke. They read their library books. Later, while she was vacuuming the bedroom, Mrs. Skeritt tried to see her family as some stranger might've. The picture they made on the bus, their noses stuck in the plastic-covered books, made her laugh. But it was a good kind of laughter, nothing mean to it. Not the kind of laughing George would do, if he could see us, Mrs. Skeritt thought later, emptying the vacuum cleaner bag.

"But George never will," she said out loud. Talking to myself! she thought. I must be going loony. The vacuum cleaner bag was filled with coarse black hairs. "George must be shedding," she whispered. They'd been so absorbed that day on the bus, they'd almost missed their stop. It was one of the nicest days Mrs. Skeritt had ever had.

Mrs. Skeritt liked her job at the Mexican Inn, though it was hard work. Every day brought a new adventure. During the lunch shift, Mrs. Skeritt met Lester Pomeroy. The restaurant was always full of policemen, since it was so close to the courthouse, and one day an officer pinched Mrs. Skeritt's bottom. This made her cry, though everyone else seemed to think it was funny. Mrs. Skeritt was drying her eyes and taking off her apron to go home, humiliated, when Lieutenant Pomeroy stood up. He towered over Officer Alpanalp, who'd pinched her.

"Can't you see she ain't that kind?" Lieutenant Pomeroy said quietly, clenching and unclenching his fists. Officer Alpanalp stopped laughing. He apologized to Mrs. Skeritt without looking her in the face and scampered out of the Mexican Inn, so scared he didn't even finish his tacos. Mrs. Skeritt put her apron back on and finished her shift. When she got off work, Lester Pomeroy was waiting. Three weeks later he became her lover.

Mrs. Skeritt was still a good-looking woman, Lester said often. More high-class than the other girls. Nothing cheap about her. Mrs. Skeritt talked more like a librarian or teacher than a waitress. With Rita at home taking care of the twins, and Mrs. Skeritt in the police car loving him up, Lester Pomeroy's life was just about perfect. He was having his cake and eating it too. Lester thought he deserved it, if anybody did.

Two months later, Mrs. Skeritt turned thirty. Lester bought her a fine gold neck chain from Leonard's. Mrs. Skeritt never wore it at home, though she probably could have. George didn't notice much of anything these days. He forgot about her birthday entirely, but this wasn't on account of him changing. He'd forgotten his wife's birthday for eleven years. George didn't hold much with sentiment.

Mrs. Skeritt never told Lester about the problems she had with George, though she longed to confide in someone. She just said there were problems, but Lester never asked what they were, so Mrs. Skeritt kept quiet and enjoyed his company whenever she could. Lester made love to her for what seemed like hours in the back of the police car—and once, the night of her birthday, at the Best Western Motel—in a sweet, appreciative, and tender way that was new to her entirely. Mrs. Skeritt enjoyed it, but this didn't seem to bother Lester the way it had George, the few times she felt something while he was taking his pleasure of her. George told her to shut up and lie still until he finished, and Mrs. Skeritt did, so ashamed she thought she'd die right there. But Lester seemed to like her feeling something, moving around.

Lester was a young man, while George was old, fifty already. They did things different in George's day.

But it wasn't just the lovemaking Mrs. Skeritt liked. Looking into Lester's farm-boy face and snuggling up against his big padded chest, listening to his heart beat after it was over, made Mrs. Skeritt feel wonderfully secure and protected, as if nothing in the world could go wrong and, if it did, Lester would fix it, since he was a policeman.

This was a good feeling for Mrs. Skeritt to take home every day. It made her stronger. And strength was something she needed, because things with George were progressing, as they tend to do, by leaps and bounds.

Mrs. Skeritt no longer slept with George, but this had nothing to do with Lester. She noticed the sheets at the foot of their bed were cut to ribbons. Mrs. Skeritt eyed George's sharp claws, thought about what they could do to her legs, which were as slim and shapely as a young girl's—or so Lester told her—and shivered. She was lucky nothing bad had happened to her yet. That night Mrs. Skeritt made up the couch. The kids noticed but didn't look surprised. They knew something was wrong but they didn't know what, and Mrs. Skeritt didn't know what to tell them.

Her husband didn't say anything either, about Mrs. Skeritt quitting their marriage bed. When she went in the bedroom to get her favorite pillow, he just growled in his usual hostile way.

"I think I'll stay up and read awhile, honey," Mrs. Skeritt said, smiling brightly. "I'm a little bit jumpy. It was probably that second cup of coffee I drank."

George just glared.

"I wouldn't want to keep you up," Mrs. Skeritt lied. That night she slept like a log.

On her next day off, Mrs. Skeritt bought some rubber

sheets at a medical supply house near Harris Hospital, to protect the mattress, and a bag of used sheets at the Goodwill for George. At three for a dollar, she wouldn't mind these sheets getting shredded the way she did her good linens, which were just as nice ten years later as when Aunt Myra first bought them. They came all the way from Ireland. Mrs. Skeritt was sick, just sick, when she saw what George had done to her sheets.

None of the new sheets matched. One was green, one blue-and-pink flowered. Another had orange-and-purple stripes. Probably owned by beatniks, Mrs. Skeritt thought. "You was a beatnik before they was beatniks!" George had said once, when they were arguing. Mrs. Skeritt had cried. These beatnik sheets would be fine for hairy old George, who still refused to see a doctor, to get another job, or to go downtown to the Welfare. They hardly ever ate meat anymore, on Mrs. Skeritt's pitiful salary. She borrowed two hundred dollars from her brother to meet the house payment, which almost killed her. Jimmy gave her the money willingly, tickled pink that she'd come by, but Mrs. Skeritt knew how Jimmy lived. George never missed a chance to remind her. It made Mrs. Skeritt sick to her stomach to take the dirty tens and twenties Jimmy peeled off his roll. She'd rather lose the house than borrow from Jimmy again, though thinking about that made her sick to her stomach too.

Serves you right, George, Mrs. Skeritt thought, making the bed. George sat in a corner in the dark, smoking Luckies, knocking back Old Crow, and growling. He wore sunglasses all the time now and kept the shades pulled tight. The daylight hurt his mean red eyes. These ugly sheets, without any crispness to them, were just what old Evil-Eye Fleagle deserved, Mrs. Skeritt thought. The orange-and-purple top sheet looked so bad against the pink roses on their field of pale blue that she had to giggle, but one black look from George shut her up. She'd boiled the awful sheets before putting them on the bed, though. Mrs. Skeritt thought she owed that to George. He was still her husband, for better or worse, and Mrs. Skeritt might be sleeping on that bed one day again herself. Who could tell who'd slept on the Goodwill sheets, what kind of dirty things they'd done on them? They might even have been owned by niggers, Mrs. Skeritt thought all at once with a shudder, then corrected herself mentally: Negroes. But Mrs. Skeritt knew, logically, that she had no call to worry. Mrs. Skeritt knew Negroes seldom gave their things to Goodwill. Like her, they couldn't afford to.

Mrs. Skeritt didn't iron the sheets like she usually did. She just threw them on the bed, hot and wrinkled and nasty, as soon as they came out of the dryer.

She never slept with her husband George again.

George Skeritt's absence made life easier for his wife, and for his children too. There was less food, but meals were more fun.

"Don't talk! Eat!" George used to say, if one of them dared to make some remark. George hated small talk. He had situated the dining room table at an angle perpendicular to the television, so he could watch the evening news from the head of the table, where he sat. No one else could see the TV set. This didn't bother George. Dinner began promptly at six, when the news did, but the news hadn't been the same since they moved John Daly to ten o'clock. Mrs. Skeritt hoped this change of anchors at ABC would cause George to turn off the set during dinner, but it didn't. The Skeritts had to sit there every night, silent, while George ate his dinner and watched TV.

Now George took his meals in his room, with the pint of Old Crow Mrs. Skeritt was ordered to buy. She'd never set foot in a liquor store before. It felt all wrong. She was afraid someone from church might see her, but no one did, and Mrs. Skeritt soon got used to Majestic Liquor, where the clerks were so young and polite. It was a fair exchange, she thought, her going there, for having the TV off during dinner.

Other things changed, too. Sometimes they ate at seven o'clock or even later. On weekends, they had picnics in Forest Park. One night Mrs. Skeritt served a salad and vegetables but no main course, and nobody noticed. The kids seemed happy whatever she fixed. And when Lester figured out from some hints she'd dropped that things were difficult at home, what with George not working, that she was having trouble making ends meet, Mrs. Skeritt had plenty of groceries.

"Why didn't you say somethin' sooner, honey?" was all Lester said before driving her to the A&P and filling up her cart. When Mrs. Skeritt told him George was bedridden and wouldn't come downstairs and find him in the house, Lester took to dropping by with the groceries instead of giving them to Mrs. Skeritt after their date. Danny and Lynda met Lester. Both of them liked him a lot.

One night, Lester took them to the Cowtown Drive-In, where they saw two Walt Disney pictures. Another time, they popped popcorn at home and watched *The Wizard of Oz* on television. Mrs. Skeritt and Lester held hands on the couch. It almost felt like they were the ones who were married, though Mrs. Skeritt wouldn't let Lester stay over, what with George upstairs, and Lester didn't press her with too much conviction. They both knew it wouldn't be right.

Lester even took Danny out in the police car and let him run the siren. Danny enjoyed it, which pleased Mrs. Skeritt. She did all she could to make Danny happy. He was starting to look a little peaked, she thought. He had nightmares and came downstairs to sleep with her on the couch when George was restless and making his noises. Mrs. Skeritt didn't encourage this—she knew it wasn't healthy—but she didn't have the heart to put Danny back upstairs.

Danny wouldn't take George's dinner up either. When

Mrs. Skeritt asked him to, he'd never say no outright, just jam his hands in his blue-jean pockets and look at the floor.

"Why not, son? Don't you want to see Daddy?" Mrs. Skeritt asked the first few times this happened, holding out George's dish.

"No," Danny said.

"Why not?"

"Just don't."

Mrs. Skeritt couldn't blame Danny, considering how it smelled up there—no matter how much she cleaned or what with—like the ape house at Forest Park Zoo. She took the bowl of raw meat up herself, with George's Old Crow, or gave it to Lynda, who, at eight, was a little angel. Mrs. Skeritt had worried at first, about Lynda coming home with her mother still at work, but Mrs. Skeritt couldn't see any problems yet. So far, Lynda seemed just fine.

Things were better for all of them, without George around. Mrs. Skeritt almost forgot he was up there. When she thought of George at all, she thought of him in the past tense. As if he were already dead.

Three weeks later, George finished changing. Mrs. Skeritt came in from her date with Lester and noticed it at once. George was in the living room, playing with Danny. Lynda was in the closet. Mrs. Skeritt heard her whimpering. George hadn't noticed his wife being home. He was having too good a time.

Mrs. Skeritt edged over to the closet door.

"Are you okay, baby?" she whispered. Mrs. Skeritt heard her daughter's sharp intake of breath. "Don't cry now." She heard Lynda struggling, trying to get ahold of herself.

"Mommy! He got Danny!" Lynda said in a gush.

"Don't worry about that now. Mommy's here," Mrs. Skeritt said with an optimistic tone she didn't feel.

"Nothing's gonna get you while Mommy's here. I promise."

"Okay, Mommy," Lynda said miserably. "I locked the door. I pushed the clothes hamper up against it too."

"That's my smart girl. I'm calling Lester. You be quiet, baby. Be quiet and stay put."

Mrs. Skeritt tried not to look at George on her way upstairs, but she couldn't help it. There was no question Danny was already dead, and the things George was doing to him shouldn't bother her, but they did.

Danny's head was nestled comfortably against a blue throw pillow, as if George had tried to give him a little nap, but this attempt at being fatherly didn't fool Mrs. Skeritt. George had hurt Danny a lot before he killed him. Danny's green eyes were wide with pain and shock, his little face was covered with deep red scratches. George was under the dining room table with the rest of Danny, watching *What's My Line?* on television. John Daly had just started introducing the panelists. Every time Bennett Cerf or Dorothy Kilgallen said something funny, George thumped his heavy tail. Mrs. Skeritt heard him growl happily, like he always did when he was enjoying a meal. Maybe George was getting full, but Mrs. Skeritt couldn't count on that. Danny was small for his age, and George had always been a big eater. She didn't have a whole lot of time.

Mrs. Skeritt tippy-toed past the living room and went up to the bedroom she'd once shared with George. She noticed Danny's door was off its hinges and that just about everything in it was wrecked. Danny tried to hide from his daddy, she supposed. That was why George hurt him so much.

"Thank you, Jesus," Mrs. Skeritt said, when she picked up the telephone and heard the dial tone. For the first time ever, she called Lester at home.

Lester laughed when Mrs. Skeritt said there was a wolf on South Adams. He thought maybe she'd got into some of that reefer her brother Jimmy sold over in colored town. But when Mrs. Skeritt told him the wolf had got Danny, Lester jumped in his squad car and headed south. One thing sure, Mary Ella loved them kids. Not a wolf though, Lester thought. No wolves in this state. But a big dog, gone bad, could kill a boy Danny's size. A pit bull or Doberman. It happened all too often. How the dog had got in was another story. Danny had probably let it in himself, to feed it. Danny was a good kid—*had* been. Kindhearted. The same age as the twins, Lester thought, stepping on the gas. This was just about gonna kill Mary Ella.

Mrs. Skeritt heard the siren a few minutes later. She heard six gunshots, louder than thunder. Then she heard Lester scream and scream.

Mrs. Skeritt ran down the stairs. As she passed the china cabinet, she picked up the first heavy thing she saw: one of the silver candlesticks Aunt Birdie had bought for her wedding. But George didn't like eating by candlelight. He liked to see what was on his plate. The candlesticks had never been used, though Mrs. Skeritt kept them brightly polished. By the time she reached the living room ten seconds later, Lester Pomeroy was already dead.

When Mrs. Skeritt saw Lester with his throat ripped open, his warm blood gushing in spurts like the beat of his big strong heart, and looked at George sniffing Lester like a rambunctious puppy, ready to chow down, something in Mrs. Skeritt snapped. It just didn't seem fair for Lester, who'd given so much pleasure, to be dead, and for George to be still alive. George had gnawed on Danny's head awhile, then spat it out like a chicken neck. Now he was drooling all over her carpet, his long red tongue dangling to the floor almost. George was still hungry. There was a lot of meat on Lester. Mrs. Skeritt stepped in front of Lester's body and kicked her husband George on the nose.

"Goddammit, George Skeritt, get out of this house!"

she yelled. Yelling at George felt good, she realized. She wished she'd done it years ago. "Go on! Git!" Mrs. Skeritt commanded, kicking him again.

George backed away from Lester's body, cringing automatically at the familiar wifely tones—familiar from the wives he saw on television programs, like Alice Cramden and *I Married Joan*. His own wife had never dared to talk like that. Not in George's very own house.

When Mrs. Skeritt opened the door to let George out, cold white moonlight caught her full in the face. She shaded her eyes with a cupped hand and looked up through spread fingers. The moon was unnaturally bright, she thought. Like the searchlight on a police helicopter.

George didn't move. He ran his tongue over his nose experimentally. The kick hadn't hurt him. He was more confused than anything else. George had never heard his wife cuss before, and the cussing caught him off guard. She's mad all right, George thought ruefully, wondering what Mary Ella mad after all these years might mean. Then George Skeritt smiled, remembering something important. Something about his new station in life.

When George leaped for her throat, Mrs. Skeritt was so astonished she struck out, to protect herself. It was reflexes, but she caught George a good one, right above his left eye. It was lucky for Mrs. Skeritt, and Lynda too, that Aunt Birdie hadn't scrimped and bought silver plate, and that Mrs. Skeritt hadn't let George put the candlesticks in their last garage sale the way he'd wanted. Mrs. Skeritt had put her foot down about that.

George looked at his wife, bewildered and hurt. His proud plumed tail drooped pathetically. Something ain't right here, George thought miserably, feeling blood in his eyes. That big cop's bullets had gone right through him. Scrawny Mary Ella couldn't be hurting him now. They hadn't said nothing about that.

Too stunned to move, George tried diplomacy. He tried to tell Mrs. Skeritt it was God's will for a man to be king of his castle and master over his wife and children. That they were his property to use as he saw fit. But all that came out was a low, mournful howl, like George was baying at the moon. While George was thinking what to do next, Mrs. Skeritt hit him again, right between the eyes. And this time George Skeritt went down.

Mrs. Skeritt straddled her husband and kept on hitting, but killing George was hard work. That awful wet thud was the worst part of it, she thought, wanting it over. Blood splattered her white uniform every time she struck. But the uniform wasn't too clean to begin with, and George's blood wasn't all that different from the salsa left over from dinner, exceptin' there was so much more of it. Blood was tricky to get out, unless you washed while it was wet, or used one of those expensive new detergents. Mrs. Skeritt doubted she'd have time to do a wash tonight. She would have to buy a new uniform, out of her own pocket, if she wanted to keep her job at the Mexican Inn.

George didn't change back the way he was supposed to. It wasn't like the movies she'd seen on TV. There was no puff of smoke and then George on her carpet with his head bashed in, looking repentant and even grateful to be out of his misery. Mrs. Skeritt was glad George didn't change back. It made explaining things a whole lot easier.

"Thank you, George dear," Mrs. Skeritt said softly, though she knew her husband didn't do it for *her*, to save her from the electric chair or Women's Prison or the booby hatch up to Wichita Falls. But Mrs. Skeritt and George had been man and wife. She wanted them to end on a positive note.

All at once George opened his mean red eyes and glared. The eyes hadn't changed a bit, unlike the rest of him. And Mrs. Skeritt knew George wasn't thanking her any, for killing him and saving his immortal soul.

He was mean clear through. Mrs. Skeritt struck again, as hard as she could. This time her husband George died.

After she called the ambulance for Danny and Lester, Mrs. Skeritt called the SPCA, to come and get George. They were real nice about it, over the phone. Then she got Lynda out of the closet.

# Baldwin County

Mr. Henry Stumpf was the richest man in Baldwin County. In 1939, he took my little sister Jess. He weighed three hundred fifty-four pounds.

He came in a limousine, black, a Packard. A big nigger drove it. The nigger wore a hat and a suit with gold buttons and braid on the shoulders, like a soldier.

Paw scratched his head when he saw Mr. Stumpf. He said, You promised you'd wait till she be fourteen.

Mr. Stumpf laughed and shook all his chins. Gotta clean her up first, don't I, John? he said. He made Jess turn round and round. He touched her delicate on the shoulder with his little fat hands, like she would break. Mr. Stumpf didn't know her. Jess could whup any boy in the county. She wore a feed sack, like Maw and Meemaw, but more careful cut, took in, embroidered around the neck.

When Mr. Stumpf saw Maw and Meemaw rocking on the porch, too fast, he tipped his straw hat and said, Howdee-do, Miz Crenshaw! Gran'mammy Hearst! then turned back to Paw with a horse-trading smile. He said, I aim to fatten her up some. I figure that'll take two year at least, scrawny as she be. Mr. Stumpf lit up a tailor-made and offered one to Paw, who took three.

Meat's sweeter, nearer the bone, Paw said.

Mr. Stumpf laughed, said, I aim to send her to school, so she don't embarrass me none.

Paw raised a big old eyebrow. Mayhap she ain't ready, he said. Mr. Stumpf tossed a twenty-dollar gold piece in the air once, twice, like George Raft, then flipped it toward Paw. Paw caught the coin, bit it with his storebought teeth, then pocketed it quick, before anybody could change their mind. Git on in the car, gal, was what Paw said to Jess. Maw held out her arms. Jess ran to them. Maw stroked her yellow hair.

What he want Jess for? I whispered to Paw.

Not to chop cotton, Paw said loudly. Then he laughed. As usual, it was an ugly sound. Mr. Stumpf gave a look that shut him up fast. Why, to marry her, boy, Paw said in a voice he stole from the preacher.

Mr. Henry Stumpf said, You comin' or not, gal? Maw dropped her arms away from Jess, who didn't wait or say good-bye. She scrambled off the porch and into the car. The windows went up like magic. We couldn't see nothing through the glass.

After the Packard was gone, the dust in the road all settled down again, Maw went out to the privy and cried. I listened through the crescent moon. Then Maw put on her hat and her Sunday go-to-meetin' dress and stuffed her things in a feed sack. She said, John Crenshaw, you sold your daughter for a mess of pottage.

'Tweren't no pottage, said Paw. 'Twere cash money! Maw shook her head. Paw said, What you think we been livin on, these past three year? The air? Who you think pays our bill to the store, since he first set eyes on Lady Jess? Why you think we hain't been flung off this place? Who been absorbin' our losses? he said. But Maw's loss was Jess.

I suppose I should be grateful, she said, that you sold her to a rich man. When Maw said this, Paw swole up proud and strutted around the porch like a rooster. I suppose I should thank the good Lord you didn't sell her to a drummer, or trade her for a jug of corn, or ruin her yourself.

Paw said, Hold your tongue now, woman!

I guess she was too fast for you, John, Maw said mildly. Where you want to stay, John Junior? she asked me then, all businesslike. Here? Or with Uncle Abner in Selma? You're big enough to pick for your own self.

Paw was giving me the evil eye. If I said Selma, which weren't no paradise nohow, he'd keep me here anyway to do for him, then whop me. Maw couldn't stop him. We all would get hurt. When he was sober, like today, I couldn't outrun him like Jess could. Maybe if I stayed, he'd sell me to a rich man too. Being sold couldn't be worse than doing for Paw. So I said, Here with Paw, like it was my choice, trying to make the best of a bad situation. Maw looked disappointed, but she wasn't thinking about me. Jess was the one she loved. She said maybe later I'd want to come along to Selma, but both of us knew I wouldn't. Maw give me a quarter when she kissed me goodbye. For the picture show, she said. Meemaw give me some bluebonnet seeds, but the color on the packet was faded. Then she and Maw left, clinging to each other and carrying on fit to beat the band, big tears splashing in the dust, all the way down the road. When they was gone for good and the dust had settled, Paw took the quarter. He let me keep the seeds, since they was old and useless. I didn't know how to find Selma by myself.

I couldn't understand what all the fuss was about then, but I understood directly, once I thought it over some, why Jess weren't just plain lucky the day she drove away in the Packard. Mr. Henry Stumpf had a wife already, Eulalia. He couldn't marry Jess, not legal, not in church. He meant to make Jess his whore. That was why Maw left Paw.

In the fall, I went back to school. Paw tried to stop me but I outrun him, since he was drunk all the time on

Mr. Stumpf's money. At school, I looked for Jess, but she weren't there. I figured Mr. Stumpf lied about schooling her, just like he lied about the marrying part. With Maw gone, nobody plowed nor planted. The home place went to rack and ruin.

Once a month, Mr. Stumpf's nigger brung us groceries from town, flour and fatback and rice and beans. I couldn't believe Mr. Stumpf would trust a nigger alone in that car. But he kept it purty and shiny, inside and out.

The nigger's name was Gladiola. The first few months, we didn't say nothing. He just handed me the groceries and drove away. He never called me nothing but boy. If Paw was home, he called him Mr. Crenshaw. But Paw never were to home. I remembered what Paw said to Maw once, when she tried to get him to work instead of drinking, tried to shame him into it. (Shame *Paw*?) Paw said, Where's my get up and go? I tell you, woman. *My get up and go just got up and went.*

I put the groceries away. If I wanted to eat, I cooked them. One day the nigger asked me about that. How you all making out, he asked, with no womenfolk to do for you?

All right, I said. A nigger shouldn't talk so intimate about white folks' doings, but I figured he meant well. It didn't rile me none. Besides, he was bigger'n me.

Then the nigger said, What you call, boy?

I said, John Junior.

He said, I is call Gladiola! Said it proud. I couldn't help but laugh. Do you know what a gladiola is, boy? I said no. He said, It is the sweetest, purtiest flower that ever did be. It grow in town, in white folks' gardens. That why my mama name me that.

I hooted out loud. Because you such a sweet, purty flower? You as big and ugly and stinky as anything I ever seed! Gladiola looked sad. I kept laughing, he kept looking sadder. I felt bad, even if he was just a nigger. Aw, don't take on that way, I said. I hadn't oughta said that about him being stinky. Niggers is sensitive about their smell. What if he stopped fetching the groceries? Don't get your balls in an uproar, I said.

Gladiola laughed then. Never heard a little white boy talk so filthy.

Never heard a big nigra talk so proper, I said. And then we was friends, even if his mammy did take his name off'n the flour sack.

One day I asked Glad did he ever see Jess. He say Jess who? I say Jess my sister. I don' know no Jess, Glad said. Ain't no Crenshaws over to Thousand Oaks. I dug my toes in the dirt. Maybe I even shed a little tear or so, wondering what Mr. Stumpf had done to Jess, whether he sold her to somebody else entirely or fattened her up like he said he was planning, then cooked her in the oven and ate her like Hansel and Gretel's witch. Maybe Jess was part of Mr. Stumpf's fat.

Glad let me stew awhile. I do know a Miss Jessica, Glad said finally with a big white grin. Gladiola still had all his teeth, unlike Paw. He was downright handsome, for a nigger.

I ain't ever heard o' no Jessica, I said, all sulky-like, though I knew Glad was trying to tell me something, to be a friend.

Too bad you don't know no Miss Jessica, he said. Couldn't be your sister nohow, so dark and ugly as you-all are. This girl be pretty as an angel, with long yaller hair.

I said, That be Jess, my sister.

Glad said, Ha! She be an orphan! Mr. and Miz Stumpf, they done taken her in.

I said, She ain't no orphan atall, she be my sister. She was born right here, right here on this place. Mr. Stumpf took her, said he gonna marry her up one day.

Gladiola whooped and slapped his knee. He said, Mr. Henry got a wife already! And Miz Eulalia be as mean as they come. She ain't got no plans to be givin' him up, and Mr. Henry hain't no Mormon infidel! He hain't no African chief! Glad did a dance, whoopin' and hollerin' around the porch. Then he stopped and wiped the tears out of his eyes. He can't be marrying *two*, Glad said.

I said, He said it just the same, said it right here in this here yard. I pointed to the dirt and stamped my feet.

Gladiola looked sad. Saying and doing be two different annimules, he said.

In April, I made Gladiola take me to Jess. You gonna lose me my job! he said. You gonna get me horse-whipped. But I had enough on him, by then, to make him. Glad had tole me all his secrets, and some of Mr. Henry Stumpf's besides. Glad had tole me quite a lot he shouldn't have. And one day I found a bill in the box of groceries Glad delivered. Reading surely does come in handy sometimes. Only half the things on the bill were in the box. It was the first use I ever got from schooling. Glad had been skimming off our groceries for a year. Mr. Henry Stumpf might not care, but if'n I told Paw, who always complained, every month, about Mr. Stumpf's stinginess and how he was holding out on us, and how fair is fair, a trade is a trade, you gets what you pays for, and so on and so forth, while he kicked me acrost the yard for a worthless book-learned ingrate and told me to go on now, git, to go pick up a mess of poke salad, or shoot a varmint, or rustle up some crawdads down to the crick to supplement Mr. Stumpf's lousy no-account groceries, Paw would kill Glad stone dead.

The reason I made Glad do it was I finally figured out what marrying meaned. I shoulda known it sooner but I didn't. It never clicked in my brain that marrying meaned that barnyard stuff. Not for Jess and Mr. Henry Stumpf. But at school I saw a comic book about Fatty Arbuckle that Joss Sanderson stole from his daddy's garage. He was so fat, his thing was so fat, the girl under him was so little and skinny, it just about made me wanna puke.

You know he killed her? Joss said, real quiet-like, after he had showed me the book.

I said, You a liar.

Joss said, No, he killed Miss Virginia Rappe with his big ole thing. He squashed her flat as a pancake. That's why they ain't no more Fatty Arbuckle movies. (I never seed no Fatty Arbuckle movies. I thought he was made up, like Popeye.) It says so, right here in this book, Joss said, before I punched his lights out.

I said, Don't believe everything you read—tearing the book up in little pieces, stomping on it.

Now what'd you have to go and do that for? Joss said. That book weren't even mine. *Goddam cropper! Goddam trash!* I punched him again. My daddy find it gone he'll skin me alive, baby Joss whined from acrost the playground, where he had run to. I shook my fist at him. Joss ran all the way home.

*Fat man, fat thing, flat sister*, was all I could think of. I thought about it running home, I thought about it getting supper, I thought it eating, I thought about it in bed. I thought about Jess under Mr. Henry Stumpf. I thought about her flattened like a frog in the road, like the ones Glad killed when he came to bring the groceries, their red insides leaked out onto the dirt, with bluebottle flies all around. Glad got out of the Packard and picked 'em up after they dried. He flung 'em acrost the field like skimmers in a crick. But since Glad was still talking about this fine Miss Jessica, and how pretty she was and how she embroidered and played the piano, and how she read books out loud to old Mrs. Stumpf, and how Mr. Stumpf took her shooting, my sister Jess must still be all right, that is if they were one and the same. I thought they were. They *must* be. And if Jess wasn't squashed flat, like the girl who married Fatty Arbuckle, she hadn't married Mr. Henry Stumpf. Not yet. He was still fattening her up. I still had time to save her.

Glad dropped me off half mile from Thousand Oaks. You never saw such a frightened nigger. He almost wouldn't take me anywhere, never mind what I had on him, once he saw I was toting Paw's gun. What you gonna do with that, Mr. John? It made me feel proud, hearing his voice shake like that, and him calling me mister. It made me feel like a man. Glad said, You hain't gonna hurt her none?

Naw, I said. I'm just gonna jaw with her some. Then I'm gonna fetch her home. Glad shook his head. I rode in the back of the Packard, just like Glad was my driver instead of Mr. Henry Stumpf's. Glad didn't know it, but I trained the gun on his neck, just in case.

Glad told me about the pasture where Miss Jessica rode her pony. After he dropped me off, I walked there, staying in the ditches, but no cars came by. Nobody saw me. The grass was cut like the golf course in the W. C. Fields picture where the golf club turns to rubber and ducks fall out of the sky. There were white picket fences and lots of horses. No mules, though. No crops growing. Flowers all along the fence. I wondered if they were gladiolas. I saw a fat white pony come trotting acrost the lawn, and a yaller-haired gal in a red velvet coat, and funny pants all puffy 'neath the fanny, and she came on toward me and then she was Jess. She rode right to the fence and stared straight at me.

Jess said, What do you want, boy? I didn't recognize her voice at all.

I said, I hain't no boy, I'm your big brother John! On that pony, Jess looked taller than me.

Do you want to play? she said. She sounded like somebody in books.

I said, Jess, don't you know me?

Jess tossed her head. My name is not Jess! That's such a common name! If'n she hadn't been up on that pony, she would've stamped her little foot.

Then what is it then? I said, remembering how much I loved her.

She said, Jessica.

Jessica then, I said. Jessica. I hated saying it. I come to fetch you home, Jessica.

Jess laughed. She said, *This* is my home, then wheeled the pony and took off acrost the field.

I crawled through the fence and hauled A after her. I was hollering, Wait up, Jess, wait up! but she didn't till I said, Wait up, Jessica. And then she slowed down to a trot. I talked sweet to her finally, the way she wanted, and pretty soon it was a slow walk and I caught up to the pony which she told me was called Peanut and we were walking along chitchatting, and as quick as Bob's your uncle we were down a hill and alongside this tiny crick, all silver and mossy and dark, and I tied Peanut to a weeping willow and Jess waited for me to help her down even though she was well able to dismount just about anything on her own, but I did it anyway, since it was part of her game. I put my arms around her and set her down.

This is where Henry takes me shooting, she said.

And when we were lying down by the tree kissing soft the way we used to, Jess said in her normal voice, What did you bring the gun for, Johnny?

And I said, I brought it in case anybody tries to stop me when I fetch you home.

And she said, The only one who'll be stopping you is me. And I saw it plain as day. She was rich and clean and happy. She did not want to be poor and sad and dirty and always doing for Paw and getting hit. I saw and I could not blame her.

But I didn't know how to raise the marrying issue, the issue of her being squashed flat, like the flowers Maw pressed in her Bible. I thought when I explained things to her, scientific-like, Jess would surely come along willingly. She would not risk being flattened like Fatty Arbuckle's wife under Mr. Henry Stumpf's great heaving stomach, but when I finally got it out she said, Oh, Johnny, you fool! Don't you know there are lots of ways to do it? The man doesn't always have to be on top. I ride him, just like I do Peanut. I'll show you, Jess said, and she got up on me, but I felt sick, like the time I saw that comic book. I hit her. Jess looked surprised there for a second, sitting in the dust on her pretty butt, her fancy pants half unbuttoned. Then she wiped the blood off her mouth with a clean white handkerchief and smiled. Johnny, you are such a child, she said.

I heard horses, and soon Mr. Henry Stumpf was there with Glad the traitor close behind, but Glad could not sit a horse. He was so funny. I laughed and laughed and laughed.

I shot Mr. Henry Stumpf, but he did not die. When he could walk again he came to see me in jail. He said, Why'd you do it, boy?

I said, You know why. He nodded. I said, You ruint my sister.

He said, No, boy. She was ruint afore I got her. She was already fair broke in. Not that it matters. I love the gal. I aim to do right by her. My word is my bond. But when the judge comes, boy, I wouldn't say nothing 'bout ruint, less'n you want to open a brand-new can of worms. Less'n you want to hurt Jess, he said. I didn't.

At the trial, Mr. Henry Stumpf pleaded my case, such as it was. The shyster lawyer didn't even try. He said I was misguided, what could you expect with a fambly such as mine. Paw, Maw, Meemaw—nobody came to stand up for me. And Jess was not there neither. They took her words down somewhere else, so she did not have to appear and get "traumatized," whatever that is. She told her tale, such as it was, and it was the truth too, more or less.

Glad told me all about her, when he come to the jail to visit, without his uniform on. Despite taking Mr. Henry to where I was with Jess, he had still been fired, but he wasn't sorry, he said. When I tried to beg his pardon, Glad laughed. He had got a job with the TVA that paid him twice as much as working for Mr. Henry. He told me they had sent Jess back east, to some school. For finishing, Glad said. To make a lady out of her. On my behalf, Mr. Henry Stumpf asked for mercy, which was what I got.

I went to the Baldwin County Home for Wayward Boys. It was not so bad. They left me alone there, mostly. The grub was better than what I could cook myself, back home. I read a lot. I finished high school. Nobody wrote me except Maw, once, to tell me Meemaw had died of grief, because of Jess and me, and Glad, to say Miz Eulalia Stumpf had fell down the stairs on Christmas Day and broke her scrawny ole neck, and Mr. Henry had married Jess right after like he promised. She wore white at the wedding, Glad said. He said she looked beautiful, just like a lady, but Jess always did, even in feed sacks. Glad said Peanut, the pony, had also died. Just keeled right over, stone dead.

When the war broke out, they turned me loose. I fought good, for a backwoods 'Bama boy, or so everybody said. I did real good for a peckerwood cracker. I learned there were lots of ways to do it too, not just with the man on top.

I got one letter from Jess, during the war, postmarked New Orleans, Louisiana, telling me about Glad, since the two of us was friends. Her husband, Mr. Henry Stumpf, had killed him, Jess said. 'Tweren't on account of me, or "our situation," as she put it so delicate-like, in quote marks. I mustn't blame myself. Mr. Henry Stumpf had been liquored up and wanted Glad's sugar ration, since his own was long used up of course, "Henry always did like his candy." And Gladiola, working for Monsanto like he did, after the TVA had finished up, and pulling down a damn good salary, married, with his own home and younguns, *on his own front porch*, said no. No! To Mr. Henry Stumpf, when he said, Come on, you give it up now, Glad. So Jess's husband shot Glad down on his porch, in front of his wife and chilluns, where he bled to death, like a dog. He rifled Glad's pockets, found the ration book, and took it and went on his way, to buy sugar. Of course there was no trial, since there were no witnesses to speak of, only Glad's wife, Lucretia, and his daughters, Violet, Peony, and Rose. Jess watched it all from their brand-new Packard. She never even got out of the car. I never knew a man loved sugar so much, Jess said. That night, she made him divinity. She was sorry, but "a wife cannot testify against her husband."

Cannot be *made* to testify against her husband, said Lafferty, who'd gone to law school in Chicago, after I read him the letter, somewhere in France.

I said, Huh?

Lafferty said, That's the law. Cannot be *made* to. The wife has the option. She could've testified, if she'd wanted to. She could've fried his ass, man. It's an excuse. Don't you get it? I didn't. I guess I *am* a fool, like Jess once said.

When I come home to do for Paw like before and put some store-bought flowers on Gladiola's grave, I met Glad's wife, Lucretia, at the nigger cemetery. Lucretia said Glad always spoke of me fondly, and how was we all doing, anyway, way out there in the country, without no womenfolk?

I said we was getting by tolerable well on our lonesomes, but the next Sunday, after church, Lucretia sent Glad's youngest gal, Peony, to do for us. Sometimes Peony brings a cake or pie. She won't take a penny for the cleaning. I try to pay her. Peony just laughs, showing Glad's good teeth.

When Peony leaves in the evening, Paw never thanks her. He never says nothing to her atall. For a while he called her names, but I broke him of that directly. Paw is not the man he was. He sits by the fire and watches her like an old bull 'gator, eyes full of rut. When I catch him looking like that I say, Me oh my, time to clean the shotgun.

Again? Paw says. He spits, gets up loud and complaining—That's the cleanest shotgun in Baldwin County—then goes outside and sits on the porch in Meemaw's rocker.

I watch Peony and oil the gun. She hums while she works with her strong tiny hands. She has purty ways. It pleasures me to see her, but my heart is pure. Not like Paw's. When Paw talks foul, Peony blushes. And this is what I think but do not say: Peony is a dusky rose.

Six weeks ago, Mr. Henry Stumpf died. His heart, they said. It just give out. Maybe Jess rode him to death, like she did that Peanut. There was no other heirs. Jess inherited all his property. She is the richest woman in Baldwin County. She bought Maw a divorce from Paw, and a house on the Bon Secour River, but I have never been there. Maw has never asked me.

Paw tried to see Jess, after Mr. Henry Stumpf died. He went to the big house and banged on the door. To get what's rightfully mine, he told me before he left. To get what's coming to me. My *due*. But it was not to be. Jess would not see him. Thousand Oaks was closed to him, tight as a drum, but Paw was liquored up and would not go away. Finally Jess called the sheriff, who hauled Paw off, kept him in town overnight, and gave him a talking to. Paw said he told him Jess—that is, the young widow Stumpf—was an orphan and didn't have no paw! And Paw could not prove otherwise neither, since Jess nor me was never registered down at the courthouse, like normal folks. Paw was too cheap. He wouldn't pay the dollar. And no one will stand up for him, not me, not Maw. No shyster lawyer will take his case. Paw won't say nothing about it no more. He never mentions Jess except to cuss her.

The night Paw was in jail, Peony cooked ham, grits, and red-eye gravy. We ate together at the table. Then Peony sat by the fire and sewed while I read to her. We read *Wuthering Heights*. Peony saw the picture of it, but I did not, for I was in the home. We had us a fine time, but quiet, like married folk are supposed to but never do, so far as I know. Peony did not stay past ten o'clock. I did not ask her to neither.

The next morning, near dawn, before Paw got out of

jail, a big black limousine came down our road. This time there was a white man driving it. I met him on the porch. He tipped his hat. He gave me a sweet-smelling envelope, pink, which I did not open. Will there be an answer, sir? he said with a stuck-up Limey accent, like I probably couldn't read nor write atall. Would you care to reply? he said.

I tore the letter in quarters and handed it back. He got in the car and started it, then pulled out slow, to keep the dust down and off of the car. I thought I saw Jess through the glass.

# For Artists Only

Jana Ann Mulcahey painted seventeen paintings at the Michigan Psychiatric Institute during her six months as a patient. She regarded the time she spent there, after being committed by her mother in cooperation with the Maryland Department of Corrections, as the most productive of her life. After she convinced the doctors to take her off Thorazine, Jana began to paint with a dedication and vigor she failed to apply to "getting well," as everyone called it.

Jana had everything she needed at MPI. She plundered newspapers and magazines for her collages and thought tearing out the images instead of cutting them with scissors, which she was not allowed, improved rather than hurt her work.

"The exigencies of chance," she'd say, pleased with the subtle textures created by the torn edges, the eager way the newsprint of the *Detroit Free Press* soaked up her cheap water-based paint. Jana was proud that she'd been able to work within the limitations of her new environment, to turn a handicap into art.

Jana's mother had brought her art supplies from the studio in Washington—except the palette knives, of course—and every Sunday Jana gave her a list of things to buy, so her mother could feel useful. But Jana didn't really need much.

That the rest of her family never came to see her didn't bother Jana, though it hurt her mother enormously. Mrs. Mulcahey was outraged at this abandonment of her eldest daughter. The Mulcaheys almost ended their thirty-year marriage over it. But this was kept from Jana, like so much else.

"She did it in cold blood," Mr. Mulcahey would explain, when his wife tried to talk him into visiting.

"I don't want to hear it!" Mrs. Mulcahey would say, putting her hands over her ears.

"You don't want to hear the *truth*, Mary."

Mrs. Mulcahey thought Jana had enough on her conscience without being bothered with family troubles, and if she was wrong there was no way she could know it. She made excuses for the rest of the family every Sunday for six months. Jana tried to stop her, but her mother always felt obligated to go through this ritual, so Jana made the appropriate noises until her mother played out and got on with the visit, which both of them enjoyed a lot. Jana and her mother had never talked much, but now they found they had things to say, though they never discussed what her mother referred to as "my baby's plight," which suited Jana just fine. The constraints that bound them improved their interaction, Jana thought with satisfaction. There were lots of advantages in being committed. Most of the time Jana was perfectly content.

It was a good thing she liked it so much at MPI, Jana thought, because the way things were going with the doctors, she might be there forever.

"Now, Mrs. . . . . Stroup?" Dr. Addison began, as he did every week.

"Please don't call me that," Jana interrupted wearily for the twentieth or so time. If Dr. Addison couldn't remember this one simple thing about her, she doubted he could remember any of the other things she'd told him either, let alone make sense of them. He seemed to remember only the things he managed to scribble in his notebook, the comments the nurses made on Jana's chart.

Why he didn't write down the name she preferred, to make things easier, *friendlier*, for both of them, Jana never would know.

"Please call me Miss Mulcahey," she said.

"Not Ms?" Dr. Addison tried to joke. Then, since no one else was going to, he laughed, as he always did. "Ho, ho, ho!" he actually went.

Jana could barely manage a tiny smile, much less a hearty, read *healthy*, laugh of her own. She recalled a line she'd read about the film *Koyaanisqatsi*. "It gives one the not unfamiliar feeling of being condescended to by idiots." Jana nodded imperceptibly. Exactly. Jana had always wanted her paintings to be as elegant as that sentence, which had convinced her to save her five dollars when *Koyaanisqatsi* came to the Tenley Circle in Washington. She giggled. Dr. Addison looked up hopefully.

"Just *Miss*," Jana said politely.

"All right. All right then. *Miss* Mulcahey," the doctor said. "Let's get on with it." And they did. By the time the so-called analysis was done, Dr. Addison wouldn't be laughing. In fact, as Jana once overheard him say, the "Stroup girl" was one of his most frustrating patients.

The problem with Jana—not just for Dr. Addison and the penal system but for her mother, too, and the family that could not even bear to see her—was that she never would admit she'd done anything *wrong*. And in her eyes, she hadn't. Her little experiment had worked out just fine. The new paintings were evidence of that. She felt absolutely no remorse.

"I did what I had to," Jana explained patiently. She was nothing if not strong-willed. *Stubborn as a goddam mule*, her husband Keith used to say.

"To improve my *work*," said Jana.

"Lack of affect!" Dr. Addison scrawled on her chart. Mrs. Stroup had a classic sociopathic personality. He felt he was getting somewhere when Mrs. Mulcahey told him Jana had never cried as a child. But when he questioned her about this, he hit another brick wall. Jana hardly remembered her childhood at all, except to note that it had been pleasant. Mrs. Mulcahey was no help either: in her opinion, Jana had been perfect—bright, beautiful, obedient, talented—right up until the day of her arrest.

Jana wanted to talk about art, but art meant nothing to Dr. Addison. Jana realized that until she knuckled under and made up a few juicy stories about how her father or, better yet, her mother had abused her or offered some convincing justifications for her behavior, she was going no place fast.

She had resigned herself early on to the possibility that she might have to stay in the mental hospital for the rest of her life. The food was hideous, but Jana had never cared about food. No one thought she was a danger to anybody, including herself, so she had ground privileges. Both patients and staff were kind, if not particularly stimulating. The important thing was that her painting was going so well, better than it ever had. Being at MPI, having nothing else to do, was good for her work, an unexpected plus. MPI forced her to develop the discipline she'd lacked on the outside. Jana thought of it as a kind of art colony, though she had never been to a real one. She had longed to go and had applied to several. She had never gotten in.

Two years ago, when she was free and leading a normal, unremarkable, and thoroughly boring life, Jana was getting nowhere with her painting. In Washington, in 1982, artists were turning Japanese, like the song said, and Jana was turning Japanese, too, though she didn't like to think of it like that. She liked to think it was her own original idea that a few dozen other people just happened to pick up concurrently, though something deep inside her continued to protest that this was not the case. Jana had a real affinity with Japan: the order, the coolness, the sense of ritual, discipline, and continuity. She hated the way Japan was seeping into American culture, where it clearly did not belong. She especially hated the clothes of Rei Kawakubo.

"What Japanese woman ever wanted to be 'like the boys'?'' Jana would fume to whoever would listen. The sharp division between the sexes, the rigidly demarcated roles for each, always complementary and never changing, never wreaking havoc or even admitting the possibility that havoc existed, was one of the things Jana found most admirable about the Japanese. The torn and formless Comme des Garçons rags that fashionable women in Washington were beginning to acquire revolted her. This was not just because the clothes were ugly, which they were, but because the people wearing them thought they expressed the essence of Japan, which they didn't. They expressed the *antithesis* of Japan, as Jana understood it. The essence of Japan was contained in the orderly, hierarchical way the Japanese organized their factories, not in Kawakubo's clothes.

Jana conceived an irrational dislike for the diminutive designer, whom she often saw in magazines, her tiny body silhouetted against the white walls of one of her many retail clothing outlets, swathed in black, off-black, and blackish-green tatters. That Kawakubo forbade her saleswomen to wear makeup so as not to distract from her precious layers Jana found fascistic. She blamed Kawakubo for much of what was wrong with contemporary America—where ideas and cultures were digested, repackaged, and sold for a profit without ever once being understood—and, by extension, with her own artwork, an analogy that made her vaguely uneasy. The pieces Jana did in response to the Japanese invasion—collagey insets of real things combined with the hard-edged calligraphy the style demanded—felt cold and formal, without any meaning she could discern or articulate to herself, much less to others. Jana thought the problem was her life and the way she lived it, that the paintings reflected the cold, rigid depths of a soul she had been unable, so far, to thaw out. She hated her terror of emotion, her automatic retreat from new experiences and people, her absence of risk-taking and passion. And it was showing in her work again, as it always had, all her life.

She'd started with meticulous pencil drawings, thousands of tiny lines that, at a distance, turned into shadows. Her later figure studies, which anticipated the New Realism, had been judged hopelessly out of date by her teachers. But their "skill" and "promise" had won her a scholarship to art school, where she had been weaned away from confidence in her own ideas. Jana didn't blame art school for that. She blamed herself, for being weak. Then came geometrical, minimalist oils in colors that had taken weeks to mix, colors so alike that only an expert could tell they weren't identical. These had been close enough to what was then in vogue to get her out of Detroit. In Washington, she'd embraced Japan with a vengeance: the calligraphy, the flower arrangements, the stylized rising sun on the Japanese flag, the sacred Mount Fuji, so much like a child's rendering of the concept "mountain" she could scarcely believe it existed in nature. Jana signed her new paintings Jane, because she felt this shortening of her given name was sparse, elegant, minimal, and therefore quintessentially Japanese.

For the first time in her life, Jana had found a style that was both fashionable and hers. With luck and hard work she might make it, she thought. If not into the big time, this new work at the very least might get her to New York, where her paintings would be seen by some powerful art-world force like Mary Boone or Leo Castelli. After that, anything was possible.

But Jana's attempt to channel her passion for Japan hadn't produced what she'd anticipated. There was something wrong with her work. There was absolutely no way she could ignore it. And once she had isolated the problem, Jana was determined to deal with it, directly and forthrightly: to conquer it. To *improve*. At the age of twenty-eight, she set out to get some experience.

* * *

Jana worked at a downtown artists' hangout that she and a few other alienated, underpaid employees had privately dubbed the Whine Bar. The place stayed afloat financially due to the bottomless pockets of its owner and the patronage of the hip-starved bureaucrats who packed it at lunch, nibbling overpriced, pseudo-vegetarian sandwiches and salads with cute New Wave names that only the jaded regulars could decipher. The GS-16's thought the place was daringly original (which it was, for Washington) because of the artists who inhabited the small back bar at all hours and took over the entire place at night, giving the place its distinctive bohemian character and the office workers a free floor show to watch while they were slumming.

Perhaps a hundred people—black, Chinese, or old— lived in downtown Washington because they had no place else to go. Three or four dozen painters, photographers, musicians, sculptors, and filmmakers lived there by choice. Although Jana had a tiny studio a few blocks from the Whine Bar, on top of a donut shop in the National Portrait Gallery arcade, she lived alone in a small apartment in suburban Arlington, on Route 50.

Unlike most of the waitresses, Jana hated the Whine Bar regulars. She hated the fact that they never got up in the morning, for starters. They wandered in at two in the afternoon, in their wrinkled, expensive clothes, with massive hangovers. They stumbled through the door and dragged their wasted bodies on to the bar stools, copies of *The New York Times* clutched to their chests like rabbits' feet, and ordered Bloody Marys, Seabreezes, or imported beers to guzzle along with the fiery house chili, which Mary Lou Kilpatrick had once called her interior sauna, before she left to try her luck in the Big Apple only to come crawling back to Washington seven months later, trying to pretend she'd never left. The name had stuck and was on the menu.

The artists staggered in one or two at a time, moaning "Oh, my head!" and "God! It was one of those nights!", met their friends, and immediately began to get drunk. Getting drunk certainly did cure their hangovers. Jana thought all of them were incipient, if not actual, alcoholics. Their conversations during the waning daylight hours invariably revolved around the events of the previous evening: how they got to be so fucked up and whether their actions while fucked up had ruined their chances to show at the so-and-so gallery, would cost them much in legal or medical fees, or had destroyed somebody's relationship or marriage. These matters being disposed of, they would all go shopping: to a western wear store on Wisconsin Avenue rumored to have a new shipment of black Levi's, or to Loehmann's in Falls Church, where Serena Cavendish had gotten a closet full of Norma Kamalis for a fraction of their actual price. Or maybe they'd just walk down the street to Garfinkel's to ogle their universally coveted collection of Maude Frizon shoes, because a hair stylist who worked there could get them for one third off, since they were on sale, plus another 20 percent off that with her employee's discount, but only if you were a size six. The men would go to St. Vincent's or Classic Clothing for oversized stewbum coats, bowling shirts, or moth-eaten Clark Kent suits.

If there was a good movie in town—made by guilt-ridden Huns or sexual perverts, or, in a pinch, a 1950s western or *film noir*—the gang would go off and see that. Then they'd go home and pretend to work for a few hours, drift back to the bar for a late dinner, run into more friends and get drunk for the second time that day, score coke or smack from Ruby the Dyke or one of the other dealers and go to one of the upstairs studios to snort it or next door, where the hippest young junkies lived, to shoot up. Later, they would wander back into the Whine Bar, fall off the bar stools, and break their ribs.

The party at the Whine Bar went on until the bar was, theoretically, closed down, but depending on who was bartending, the actual closing would take place far later. The shades would be drawn tight, in case the <u>cops came</u>

by, and three or four diehards would still be going at it into the morning. Then they would stagger off to the holes they'd crawled out of, if they were lucky enough not to get mugged, raped, or beaten by some dark-skinned local en route.

Any attempt at discussing the effects of heroin on the body would be met with the following reply: "But Diana Vreeland *said* junkies have the best skin!" This was the last word on the subject, the ultimate conversation stopper. Looking at a whey-faced teen-aged musician, barely recovered from her third bout with hepatitis, made Jana hate Diana Vreeland almost as much as she hated Rei Kawakubo. She thought the old crocodile should be shot for that remark.

But what made Jana *really* hate the Whine Bar regulars was the way they always talked about their work while they were fucking off so devotedly.

"Got, I've got so much *work* to do," Sasha Rubin would be sure to say, just before she ordered her third Bloody Mary of the afternoon.

Harry Lee Ames would try to one-up her: "I've got that group show coming up at the Corcoran on the eleventh! I just *know* I'll never finish in time!"

"Another vodka and grapefruit?" amiable George, the afternoon bartender, would ask about then. With a mournful nod of his blond, exquisitely empty head, as if he didn't have a choice, Harry would say yes, then stick a silver spoon under George's nose, by way of a tip. Jana was the only person at the Whine Bar who actually turned down cocaine. This gave her a somewhat mythical status.

If they would only stop complaining about how much they had to do and actually do it, Jana would have respected them more. Probably she would. There wasn't much chance of her finding out. It wasn't called the Whine Bar for nothing.

The sleeping around they all did revolted her too. Their relentless trivialization of sex, Jana thought, reflected their essentially trivial natures. She knew other people considered her beautiful, that by the standards of contemporary American beauty, which she closely approximated, she *was* beautiful, but Jana had never cared about her looks. She preferred to be sought out for what she worked for and created, rather than what she'd been handed by her parents.

Practically everybody in the Whine Bar, male and female—since bisexuality was another one of their pet perversions—had tried to pick Jana up, but she had said no to all of them. All except one. She had taken Alex White home because *he* was so beautiful. His seeming decency and loneliness had appealed to her as well, but those wouldn't have meant so much without his unquestionable good looks, the wholesome All-American kind of looks Jana herself had. They looked good together, she thought, walking down the street arm in arm after leaving the bar: Alex tall and blond, like a ski instructor or a lifeguard; and she tall too, with straight red hair she could sit on. Alex said she looked like a young Jane Asher, and Jana took this as a compliment, though she couldn't really remember what Jane Asher looked like, or who she'd been, other than Paul McCartney's girlfriend.

Once Jana got Alex home and into bed, she found he wasn't so much interested in making love to her as he was in humiliating her. The transformation began the minute Alex walked in her door and was finished by the time he got his pants off. Alex never kissed her, not once. He told her what he wanted her to do to him and vice versa, almost none of which was actually accomplished. Their sex was awful and mercifully brief, but Jana was enough of an optimist to think it could be fixed if they cared enough for each other to work on it. So she decided to talk to Alex. She took his hand and kissed it tenderly, trying to start the conversation in a nonthreatening way, since she knew men were sensitive about their performance, but before she managed to say anything, Alex got up, put on his clothes, and left. He hadn't said one word to her, other than nasty four-letter ones, since he'd arrived at her place in Arlington thirty minutes earlier.

Jana couldn't believe anyone could be so cruel with so little cause. The next day, at the Whine Bar, Alex wouldn't even speak to her.

"Can we talk about it, Alex?" Jana asked.

"Talk about what?" Alex said coldly, then pulled up his feet, grabbed the bar with both hands, and pushed off hard. He swiveled round and round on his bar stool, his finger sticking out like the pointer on a roulette wheel, and stopped his spin suddenly when his back was to Jana.

"Looks like your lucky day, sweetmeat," Alex said to the girl on his left, tucking his hand into the crook of her arm and brushing his knuckles against her breast.

Jana was so confused that she had to confide in someone. She chose Ruby McGee, the daytime cook and coke dealer. Jana thought Ruby, a lesbian, would be sympathetic, and she was right. Ruby already knew she'd been to bed with Alex. Everyone in the bar knew it, from Alex's own lips. According to Ruby, Alex was a notorious creep and sadist who took his failed marriage out on any woman who'd let him. Jana was the only one in Washington, it seemed, who didn't know about Alex's problem. Usually, he hit on tourists.

"It was a real feather in his cap, honey, getting you in the sack," Ruby said longingly. Jana went out to her Toyota and cried.

Jana swore she'd never risk sleeping with another Washington artist, but there weren't a whole lot of other possibilities. The Young Republicans and Moral Majority types, in their polyester suits and second-rate prep school ties, were everywhere. She'd never met a single one of her neighbors in Arlington. And in Georgetown, a very large drunk had tried to bite her on the ass. When Jana had protested, he had told her she'd been asking for it since her jeans were so tight. She never went to Georgetown again. Jana never met anyone at all, outside of the Whine Bar.

Most of the other waitresses identified with the customers. They socialized with them, slept with them, called them friends. When they got off work, the bar became their home away from home too. They talked and laughed and ate and paid for their own drinks. They tipped well. Off work, they were all but indistinguishable from the regulars. But this graceful shifting of roles, this blurring of class lines, was alien to Jana. She felt the other waitresses were kidding themselves, aided by the downwardly mobile customers. Jana was never able to forget she had to work in order to eat, while the customers didn't, or at least not so you'd notice. That she had to listen to them all day while they had the leisure to create or, what was worse, to *not* create and then whine about it, caused a hard indestructible kernel of hatred that Jana felt every minute she spent in the Whine Bar.

Some of them had to be nice, Jana told herself. Some of them were friendly, quiet and unpretentious, talented and handsome, never drank too much, and didn't seem promiscuous. Like Alex White, Jana thought, and shuddered.

As soon as her shift was over, Jana left the Whine Bar. She never sat down to socialize, though she was often asked to. She left as soon as she could. She hated her job. Despite this she was an excellent waitress.

Jana had almost resigned herself to the fact that she might never get the experience she craved when Ruby McGee asked her to a party in Adams Morgan. Three hours later, Jana was sitting on a dilapidated couch while a huge bearded man whose name she never quite caught shoved a Quaalude into her mouth with his tongue. Perhaps this happened more than once. Later he and a friend threw Jana on a bed. Her so-called pal Ruby was nowhere in sight. Jana wanted to get away but discovered she couldn't walk. Two large pink blobs were smothering her when a thin brown blob appeared out of nowhere.

"Get off her, man, she's too fucked up," he said, but

nobody paid any attention. He plucked one of the men off Jana and slammed him against a wall. Romeo number two, the hairy one, backed off immediately.

"Hey, man. We don't want any trouble, man," Jana heard somebody say. The next thing she remembered was the cold night air hitting her and a big man holding her arm.

"My purse?" Jana said, her tongue thick enough to row boats with. The man held it up. They found her Toyota where she'd left it, in front of an Ethiopian restaurant. The man helped Jana into the passenger seat and fastened her seat belt. There wasn't a lot she remembered after that.

Jana woke up to the smell of bacon. For a minute she thought she was back home in Detroit, with her mother in the kitchen. Jana gave herself up to the pleasure of that illusion, burrowing into the pillow, smiling, secure. Then she remembered one or two things and sat up straight all of a sudden.

Her clothes were still on her. The only naked part of her was her feet. Could someone have undressed her, fucked her, then dressed her again? Unlikely. Unzipping her jeans and feeling herself with a finger, Jana concluded not. She willed her heart to stop racing and got out of bed, put her shoes on, and went downstairs, head pounding in protest to find out where she was.

The man who'd saved her was at the stove. Jana stood in the doorway, terrified. When he turned around, Jana noted through her hangover that he was easily the most beautiful person, male or female, she'd ever seen in her life. Long brown hair, buttery buckskin shirt laced halfway up, tattoos up and down both arms, piercing blue eyes. And he was *cooking*. Surely that was a good sign.

"Morning," he said, turning back to the stove.

"Morning."

"Sleep okay?"

"Uh huh."

He turned to her finally and grinned. "Don't just stand there, Red."

Jana crept over to the table and sat down. When the man banged the skillet down on the table in front of her, she jumped.

He laughed. "Hey. I almost forgot. You want some Tylenol or something?" Jana nodded. The man got the Tylenol and a jelly glass of water to wash it down with. "Think you can eat? I figure you might be a little shaky."

"I can eat," Jana said. "Where are we?"

"Hyattsville," he said.

"Hyattsville? Where's that?"

"You never been to Hyattsville before?"

"Hyattsville *where*?" The man looked puzzled. "What state?"

"Why, the great state of Maryland. You ain't from around here, are you? Didn't think so. Hey! Your eggs're getting cold."

"Is it far?"

"From D.C.? Nah."

Jana ate. She couldn't stop staring at his hands, the biggest she'd ever seen. Despite their size, they were beautiful, perfectly proportioned, the fingers long and thick. As she looked at them, Jana felt this wave of something sweeping over her which she supposed must be lust, though it was unlike anything she'd ever felt before, toward anybody. She looked up guiltily and saw him smiling, just like he could read her mind.

"Not many girls left can still blush," he said. Jana didn't know what to say. She concentrated on eating her eggs, though she didn't want them. "Not around here, anyways." He finished his breakfast in three or four quick bites, rinsed his plate under the faucet, stuck it in the drainer, and went out the door.

When the man didn't come back after five minutes, Jana dumped her breakfast in the garbage and went outside. He was on the back porch steps, whittling. For just a minute, Jana felt like she was in Appalachia. The dilapidated frame house in the middle of nowhere, the black mongrel dog, the big man whittling. Her hangover increased her disorientation. Only the sight of her own Toyota, parked next to the house, and two or three derelict motorcycles out back, anchored her to the present. She sat down beside him on the porch.

"What are you making?" she asked. The man opened his hand and held out what looked like a severed penis, about eight inches long. Jana stood up fast enough to make her head spin, wondered where in Hyattsville she could run.

"Don't worry, it ain't gonna bite ya," he said. "It ain't *real*. It's a knife handle. A lot of guys like 'em. You know. Bikers."

"Are you a biker?" Jana finally got out.

"Would you like me to be?"

"Not particularly."

"Well then, I'm not."

"I didn't think so."

"Why? What d'you think a biker is, anyway, Red? Big and fat and smelly, huh? With his belly hanging out under his T-shirt? Like in the movies, right? I *been* a biker. Looked just the same as I look right now. You believe that?" Jana smiled, nodded. He laughed. "You better! I got out a long time back. I'm not much for . . . *organ-i-zations*," he said, stringing the word out. "I ride alone, usually. You ever been on a bike?"

"Lots of times."

The man laughed again. "Lots of times, huh? I bet. I'd give you a ride, only my bike's downtown. I drove *your* car."

"Thanks," Jana said.

"Better watch them 'ludes. They don't seem to agree with you much." Then: "Hey . . . nothin' happened last night. I'm not that hard up."

"I know."

"Oh, you *know*, huh? College girl, ain't ya?" The black dog came over and sniffed Jana's crotch.

"I'm a waitress," Jana said, pushing the dog away, thinking about the Whine Bar. Already, she was late for Sunday brunch. "I've got to get to work."

"Hey," he said. "I'm Keith Stroup. What's your name, anyway?"

"Jana Ann," she said, realizing after she said it that she hadn't used her given name with anyone except her family since she left Detroit.

"Jana Ann! Hey, that's some mouthful," said Keith. "You work at that joint where Ruby works? Ruby the dyke?" Jana nodded.

"Maybe I'll come in sometime. Get me some chili," Keith said, and four days later he did.

During the month she dated Keith, Jana got lots of experience. There was sex, lots of sex, the kind that left her pleading for more, no matter how much she'd had already, and drugs that soon made her want more of them too. There were rides on Keith's bike, her arms around his waist, like the flying she did in her dreams. There was no painting, but Jana didn't worry about that. She was getting experience. The art would come later.

Jana quit her job at the Whine Bar, gave up her apartment on Route 50, and moved in with Keith. She didn't give up her studio, although she never went there. When Jana moved in, Keith told her he didn't have enough money to support them both, but Jana did nothing about finding a new job. Keith had inherited his house from his parents and made a little money fixing bikes and carving the penis-shaped knife handles. Some of them were realistic and frightening, like dildoes. Some were humorous, with smiling faces or pursed lips on their heads like kissing fish. Jana's favorite was made of ebony, and had a face on both sides: one smiling, one frowning. Jana urged Keith to keep this one instead of selling it, and to make her happy he did.

One night, a biker friend of Keith's came to visit. His

name was Harlan and he was as big as a house, his belly protruding over his belt, the crack in his ass showing under his T-shirt when he bent over to make a pool shot at the Terminal Bar. Harlan was the parody biker that Keith had ridiculed the day he and Jana met. Keith ordered Jana to sleep with him, as a courtesy. Jana said no. Keith hit her for the first time since they'd been together. Jana took off all her clothes, piece by piece, in their bedroom, and threw them in Keith's face, then walked across the hall to the spare room, to Harlan.

Harlan was so fat he was barely human. When Jana left his room, she didn't feel guilty. Why should she? She didn't feel she'd been unfaithful to Keith. She was only following orders. Keith took Jana in his arms when she came back to their bedroom, stroked her red hair gently, then fucked her with the handle of her favorite knife, like she'd always wanted him to but never said. Keith held the blade tight, so the knife wouldn't slip, especially at the juncture between ebony and steel. When it was over, Jana noticed the blood.

"Your pretty hands, baby. Your poor pretty hands," Jana kept babbling, after she found out she wasn't hemorrhaging. She kissed Keith's hands until his blood was all over her face. Keith had to hit her again to get her to stop, so he could rinse his hands off and see how bad the cuts were. He poured iodine all over them, then wrapped a towel around each hand. When he got back, Jana was still sitting there, glassy-eyed and bloody, looking like she'd been beat to shit, which made Keith angry.

"Go wash your face," Keith told Jana. When Jana didn't move Keith pushed her off the bed with his foot. She landed like Raggedy Ann.

"I said go wash your face," Keith repeated. "Then clean the sink. Move your ass, Jana Ann." When Jana didn't move, Keith decided to let it slide. He turned on the TV, just in time for the last half of David Letterman, poured himself a Jack Daniel's, and started to relax. The cuts were shallow, and Keith loved Stupid Pet Tricks.

Just about the time Keith had almost forgotten she was there, but not quite, because his hands still hurt like hell, Jana got off the floor, went into the bathroom, and did what Keith told her. She looked just fine, coming out of the shower, damp and rosy. Not a scratch on her. She smiled this sweet little smile that broke Keith's heart, then crawled into bed and put her head on his chest. When the ferret threw up all over David Letterman, she giggled, just like nothing had happened.

"You know what I found out tonight?" Keith asked after Stupid Pet Tricks ended. Jana didn't say anything, but she was listening, all right. "You know what I found out?" Keith repeated.

"What?" she said finally.

"You are one sexy lady, Jana Ann, but you're also fucking crazy!" Keith hugged her with real affection. Jana started crying.

"Hey, stop that, man!" Keith said, holding her face tight in one big hand and shaking it. "Stop it, or I'll fucking belt ya!" Jana stopped crying when she saw that Keith was kidding. "I *like* crazy people," he said.

"You do?"

"Uh huh. I like 'em a lot."

A few seconds later, they were laughing so hard they rolled off the bed. By the time Keith's cock was where his knife had been, he'd forgotten all about the cuts on his hands, and about David Letterman, completely. The towels unraveled, the scabs broke, the bed looked like a slaughterhouse by the time they finished. Then Jana was up, full of energy, like she always was after sex, emptying ashtrays and changing the sheets.

"You didn't have to do that sex bit, with Harlan," Keith lied casually, cleaning his nails with the ebony-handled knife. Jana smiled. "You don't ever have to do anything you don't want to."

Three weeks later, Keith and Jana got married. The next day, Keith put Jana on the streets. Jana knew she was wasting herself, giving blow jobs in parked cars in front of the Pink Pussycat Lounge on Connecticut Avenue. Ruby McGee's girlfriend Ginger, who worked inside and made five times what Jana made but was nowhere near as pretty, told her this, shaking her curls in dismay at Jana's stupidity. Jana knew she could rake it in as a stripper or call girl. But she liked having Keith nearby, sitting in her Toyota, watching out for her. She liked not having to wear anything fancier than cut-offs. Working cars was safe, fast, and lucrative. She didn't plan to do it for the rest of her life.

But when Jana caught something and gave it to Keith, they decided enough was enough. They held up some Chicken Delites, then a liquor store in Hyattsville, and eventually branched out to Gaithersburg. Jana drove the Toyota at first, while Keith did the inside work, but she soon got tired of that arrangement. She begged Keith to let her handle the gun. Keith indulged his wife one night on what he figured would be an easy job. He sat in the Toyota with the motor running, kissed Jana on the cheek, and watched her swing her pretty tail into Popeye's Chicken, so proud to be her husband he could bust.

Jana had always wondered how it felt to take a life. When she shot the old black man for no good reason, after he'd already put the money in the bag, Jana found out it felt like nothing at all. She was still standing there, amazed at how much like nothing it felt, when Keith came in and dragged her away. Rattled by the killing, Keith drove too fast and hit an off-duty cop, Ipana Mattheison, who died. Eventually, Keith and Jana were caught. Perhaps this had something to do with the fact that the Popeye's Chicken they'd held up was less than a mile from their home.

The lawyers Mrs. Mulcahey retained advised severing Keith and Jana's cases, and this was granted by the judge.

Keith Stroup was represented by a public defender, who only saw him once before his case went to trial. Jana was represented by the best law firm in Washington. All Mrs. Mulcahey's savings went for those lawyers. Her husband wouldn't contribute a dime. He washed his hands of Jana, he said. But the Whine Bar owner, Gerald Knight, gave a party at the Pension Building to raise money for her defense. Tiny Desk Unit, Egoslavia, and the Urban Verbs played gratis. Laurie Anderson and David Byrne might or might not have been there. A good time was had by all. When the party's costs exceeded ticket sales, Gerald kicked in two thousand dollars, out of his own pocket. Jana never said thank you, which pissed Gerald off somewhat but made a certain amount of sense, he had to admit, given her plea.

Jana was found not guilty by reason of insanity. Keith Stroup, who had a previous record, got twenty years to life.

Keith understood the way Jana had acted, the things her lawyers said about him at the trial. Keith wanted Jana to be free. He *loved* her. What he didn't understand was the love notes he never got from Jana, when he sent her so many at such cost, the tender looks they never exchanged in court, and the way Jana stared at him once, when they collided in the corridor: just like they'd never even met.

When Jana had been at MPI for six months, Dr. Addison came in with four embarrassed attendants, a triumphant smile on his face, his skin flushed dark red, and took away her paintings and art supplies. Jana tried to stop him and was put under sedation.

When Jana came out of the medication and attacked Dr. Addison, who was sitting by her bedside, the doctor believed he'd made a breakthrough. At last Mrs. Stroup was responding with strong emotion! Dr. Addison wasn't as stupid as Jana thought, and it had eventually gotten through to him that Jana was happy at MPI and therefore not inclined to respond to his therapy. It was her painting that made her content; ergo, Dr. Addison would take it away and see what happened. Mrs. Mulcahey had agreed, when Dr. Addison explained it to her. In the hall, drinking brackish coffee with the other doctors, Dr. Addison looked positively smug.

As soon as she had a chance to, Jana spread a bedsheet on the floor, sat down on it, and bit her own wrists, like a trapped coyote will chew off its paw. Several minutes later, she got up, staggered over to the right hand corner of the sheet—her bloody footprints marring the composition somewhat—and curled up to die, signing her final painting, an homage to the Rising Sun.

Since Jana had never exhibited suicidal tendencies, the doctors didn't feel *they* were to blame. Since her method of exiting the world was unique, the attendants didn't see how they could have stopped her.

Judson Dodd, an assistant curator at the Detroit Art Institute, arrived at MPI several days later to visit his alcoholic mother and saw three of Jana's paintings being tossed in a Dumpster. When he found out a dozen had already been hauled away and several more had been painted over by some patients during art therapy, Judson forgot about his mother and started to squawk, as was his wont when he was excited. He jumped in his Subaru and raced to the dump. The paintings were still there. Whistling merrily, he loaded them into his car to join the three he'd wrested from the startled MPI janitor and headed for Stop Six to visit the Mulcaheys.

Three months later, the Detroit Art Institute mounted a show entitled: "A Life for Art: Jane Mulcahey, 1955–1984." Judson was unable to hang Jana's last painting, for that, to his horror, had already been laundered and was in use somewhere at MPI, perhaps on or beneath his very own mother. But he *was* able to obtain, through his brother-in-law, Detective Wendell Crow of the Detroit Police Department, a series of photos of Jana's death. Judson had these blown up to life size, then hand-tinted.

They caused a local, then national, sensation, as did the painted-over canvas he bought from Marcella Lane, a ward attendant at MPI. Judson restored it, at great expense, but only halfway, so that the result was half Mulcahey, half Mrs. Peter Van Brunt, a lifelong resident of MPI. The psychedelic mandalas she painted in Day-Glo colors, so beloved of schizophrenics and thought by psychiatrists to be healing, obscured half of Jana's subtle collage in red, black, and gray. Undoubtedly, the defaced painting would have been a masterpiece. Some present-oriented types urged Judson to restore it all, but, thinking of the long haul, he held out. This "demi-Mulcahey" soon became Jana's most valuable work, encapsulating as it did her life, death, and art. Jana's reputation was made, and that of the "visionary Judson Dodd" along with it.

Marcella Lane lost her job at MPI for smuggling out the painting—and Jana's psychiatric records, which made up the bulk of the Art Institute catalogue—but Judson paid her well enough so Marcella didn't care. She felt like a hero, sort of, and everyone treated her like one whether she was or not, which Marcella liked better than having a full-time shit job.

Three weeks later, one of Jana's paintings was on the cover of *Time*. *Ms.* and *Artforum* also did cover stories. Keith was interviewed in prison. His comment that he didn't even know his wife could paint caused a minor sensation. Ruby McGee recounted, in lurid detail, the story of Jana's date with Alex White. Alex, Keith, and Dr. Addison were seized upon by the women's movement as three good answers to one of feminism's perennial questions.

"Why have there been no great women artists?" asked the headline in *Ms*. The montage beneath it, which juxtaposed a mug shot of Keith, Dr. Addison with his coat over his head, and Alex White coming out of the Whine Bar with a pretty tourist in tow, answered the question effectively and, one would hope, for all time.

Women Against Violence Against Women went even further, blowing their entire February budget on three hundred thousand black-bordered posters featuring Keith, Alex, and Dr. Addison. The caption, in huge black letters, said WANTED FOR FEMICIDE.

Alex knew he was finished in Washington, and all because of that Mulcahey bitch, that no-talent, that *waitress*. Alex couldn't even remember what he'd done to her that was so awful, so similar was his night with Jana to hundreds of others in his life. He telephoned his mother for money so he could escape to Europe, but Mrs. White, who could read as well as the next person in Shaker Heights, Ohio, refused to help her youngest son for the first time in her life, a decision which left her exhilarated.

Going to Europe wouldn't have helped Alex much in any case. People read *Artforum* in Europe too. So Alex hitchhiked to Mexico, where he found he could make a decent if not spectacular living painting big-eyed children and Elvises on black velvet. In Mazatlán, the women were as hot as the sun, as juicy as mangoes, and as plentiful as sand on the beach. Alex could have a different one every night, if he wanted to, and Alex did. And all without buying a single drink! Also, they eschewed back talk. What did it matter anyway? He couldn't speak a word of Spanish. Alex was happier in Mexico than he'd ever been in his life.

Although Dr. Addison was never formally charged with any wrongdoing, he was so humiliated by the brouhaha and almost universal scorn attached to his name—"Killed any more artists lately, Dr. Addison?" the *Artforum* article sneered under his photograph—that he left MPI and joined the staff of a small psychiatric hospital in Fort Worth, Texas, where the most well-known painter in town was the long dead, unquestionably male Frederic Remington. Dr. Addison found this comforting. He would have been horrified to know that his name entered the English language as a verb, because of his interaction with Jana Ann Mulcahey. The latest edition of *The Dictionary of Slang and Euphemism* defines "Addisonize" (between "Adam's own: the female genitals, British, 1800s," and "Adod! see also Adad! Agad! Ecod! and Egad!'') as "to deprive one of everything that gives life meaning, after Dr. Nelson Addison, psychiatrist." In art ghettoes throughout the land, people were screeching at their significant, albeit transgressing, others, "You've Addisonized me completely, you asshole!" But in Fort Worth, Dr. Addison never heard his name so debased. This perversion of his good name never made it that far south. In fact, Dr. Addison was happier than he'd ever been, just like Alex White was. He loved the warm weather, the spicy food, and the friendly people of Texas. He married an Irish nurse and got very fat indeed. He never thought of Jana Ann at all.

When the price of Mulcaheys hit fifty thousand per—after all, there were only so *many* of them—Judson Dodd was forced (by his wife, his detoxed mother, rumors he'd heard of an impending lawsuit, and the fact that *Artforum*, after praising him so highly, was now referring to him—in print!—as "art ghoul Judson Dodd" every time he made a sale) to return to the Mulcahey family with an offer to divide the profits from Jana's work somewhat more equitably. There was a law pending to make that de rigueur, anyhow. Judson thought he might as well compromise while it could still do him some good. The terms of the settlement are unknown. But after Judson's visit, Mr. Mulcahey sold the house on St. Mary's and bought a new one in Palmer Park, more willing to spend Jana's money than he ever was to spend his own. Johnny Mulcahey was able to quit working at the Texaco on Eight Mile and open his own auto body repair shop. And Susan Mulcahey, the youngest daughter, who called herself Suze, was able to leave Detroit for Washington and enroll in art school.

Keith Stroup was the only person, besides Jana herself,

who didn't benefit from her death, at least in some fashion.

"That your wife?" several people asked him, after the article in *Time* came out.

"Uh huh."

"Pretty girl."

"I know."

"Too bad, man." They patted him on the back and went away. Nobody in prison blamed Keith for Jana's death. Women were supposed to work for their men. What Keith had done was small stuff, compared to most. He had never really hurt her. Au contraire, as Judson Dodd might have said.

Still, the whole thing bothered him. Keith studied the reports of Jana's death in the prison library, trying to understand. If Jana was such a genius, like the magazines said, what had she been doing with him? She'd wanted him, that was for sure. He hadn't forced her into anything, certainly not into marrying him. That had been *her* idea. He hadn't twisted her arm on the rest of it either.

"Leading her into a life of crime, my ass," Keith said. She'd *wanted* to do it. All of it! The question was why. Keith never found the answer, but at least he was asking the right questions.

Poring over the Detroit Art Institute catalog, Keith was sure of one thing. The paintings she'd done after she met him, while she was in the loony bin, weren't any worse than the ones she'd painted before. He couldn't see any difference between them, and Keith had a good eye. The new paintings were just like the old ones. Any fool could see that.

In this way, Keith was able to say goodbye to his wife and hello to prison, where he would be for a good long while. Saying goodbye was hard. Keith had loved Jana.

One day he saw an eighteen-year-old with dark red hair, the same color as Jana's. Keith cut two members of the Mau Mau Nation and one Aryan Brother to get Will O'Gara for himself. The Aryan never woke up, but the Mau Maus were prowling around, laying for him. Keith thought it was worth it. Nestled against Willie's backside, listening to his regular guiltless breathing, as sweet and untroubled as a child's, Keith thought of his dead wife, whose hips had been as slim as a young boy's. His findings about her work, however, went unpublished.

# Found in a Trunk in Springfield, Ohio

1 *a large sheet of blue-lined paper. writing on both sides of the paper. heavy penciled script. an envelope addressed to Mr. J. C. Hubbard, Springfield, O.*

Detroit, Mich.
10-6-16

Dear Brother,

Rec. your kind and ever welcome letter which found us in good health and out of work for about 6 weeks now and do not know when I will get back to work. But will make out some how. There is nothing doing here in this town. But they claim Detroit is in better shape than most. There are lots of holdups now. Sat. night 2 men held up a street car and used a revolver to do the trick with. I am still trying to do what is right before God and Man and I feel better for my efforts. Brother, you would not recognize me. 5 weeks now since I took a drink and hope I will never touch it again.

Well, the weather is rainy today. But we have had 2 nice sunshiney days and they made a fellow feel good to see them.

I wish you could learn the glass business for it is a good money job but as you say an awful dangerous job. But butchering is dangerous too, tho a body would not know it to watch you use those knives. And money is not everything in this world. No matter what our work we have the risk of falling or of something falling on us. Life is uncertain. We know nothing about how long we can live or how we may die. Dot's father is at the point of death. We drove to Wheeling on Sat. evening to see him and she and the children are there yet. His kidneys are all shot to pieces and have poisoned his blood so bad that big ulcers got in there and had to be opened up. He is in awful shape, it don't look like he can last very long. I never was so glad to quit a place as the Otwells tho I did not like leaving Dot to listen to Howard's lies. If the Good Lord himself came down off his cross for Dot her brother would still find fault with him somehow, but Dot will stick to me irregardless, and soon I will have her back home.

Ferd is selling shoes downtown and Bill is getting in a little time with Ford.

Well, so long. I would like to see you. Be good and write.

Your brother,<br>Frank

2  *a large sheet of blue-lined buff paper. heavy black script with flourishes. two green one-cent stamps.*

Detroit, Mich.<br>November 18, 1916

Dear Joe—

Your welcome postal was duly received today—glad to see that you are well.

I am very satisfied with Detroit. Am working for a fine employer and make 45 cents per hour, and lose but little time even in the winter. I don't think I will ever regret leaving Springfield, for it is "no good." It is cold up here alright but I don't mind as long as I have work.

Frank was with us until a week ago when he went to Wheeling for the funeral and to carry Dot and the little ones back home. Frank had worked all summer for the Pittsburgh Plate Glass Co. and got laid off.

Guess Springfield is going to be pretty dead again this winter.

Write soon again and tell me all the news. And with best wishes for your success I remain

Yours truly
Bill

3 *the large sheet of blue-lined paper. the heavy black script with flourishes.*

Detroit, Mich.
Feb. 14, 1917

Dear Friend Joe:

Perhaps you have reached the conclusion that I have obliterated your name from my memory as it has been a long while since you heard from me but this is not the case. Business has been slow here for most but has begun to brighten in our line of work. I have been very busy, in fact you might say "working night and day"—I worked all night for three nights last week and until 2 o'c. Sunday morning. I have had all the work I could do and this is why I could not write.

Say Joe it is Ferd's and my intention to open up a grocery store here this coming Sept. and we would like to have you to go into the "Meat" business in the same building with us. You would only have to share ⅓ of the light, heat, and rent bills while the rest would be profit to you. Grocery stores are run different up here to what they are in "dear old Springfield." This is a paying business, everybody sells "strictly for cash," just as it should be. No credit goes in this town. Let us have your views and intentions concerning this matter, as we will want someone to look after this end of the business and we are giving you first option.

I believe you would like Detroit. It is a fine city to live in with lots of amusements, not like home.

Oh say Joe, where was I on the 16th? What is the difference between the difference? Ha, ha, ha. How is the Union progressing there?

I will close for this time by asking you to answer soon. I am as ever

Your old friend,
Bill

4 *the American flag printed in red, white, and blue in the left corner of the self-folding envelope. the YMCA logo on the right.* WITH THE COLORS *printed in blue block letters. the blue-lined paper. the heavy penciled script.*

Phila., Pa.
5-14-17

Dear Brother,

I have not received any news from you so I thought I would write one more time. I hope you do not feel hard toward me. I never could tell what you were thinking and still cannot if you do not make your feelings known loud and clear. It is true you saw her first but Joe, she made her own mind up, I did not force her, and fair or not, after that there was no going back. She is one stubborn girl. I know I have not been a good husband all the time but I swear I never laid a hand on her no matter what Howard Otwell says, she would not have put up with it, and anyway that part of my life is over. I will be a good husband and father too when this War is over, God willing. So please write.

Well, Joe, I will leave here for sea in a day or two. I don't know what boat I'll get but will let you know later.

This place here is a pretty big city about 1 million and 1/2. I am about 1 and 1/2 hrs. ride from New York, which am told is full of Abes. Well, Joe, if you don't hear from me before some time don't worry for I can't tell where I'll go. Good By from

> Your big brother,
> Frank Hubbard
> Baker 1st Cl.

P.S. Joe, just got word we leave tomorrow for France.

5  *the American flag in the left-hand corner of the self-folding envelope. the YMCA logo. the thin blue-lined paper. HELP YOUR COUNTRY BY SAVING. WRITE ON BOTH SIDES OF THIS PAPER printed in tiny caps at the bottom. the black script with flourishes. the writing on both sides of the paper.*

Dec. 24, 1917

Dear Friend Joe—

I beg you not to be mad at me or anything like that for not answering your letter. I just write when I get the notion. The Army makes me that way. I am one S. O. L.—"soldier out of luck." Ha, ha, ha.

Say Joe, it looks like we will go over to France alright. We are drilling hard and working hard. Boy, it would be nice if I could only get home to see you and the rest of my friends. It seems like years since I have seen you and am disappointed for I thought I would get to Springfield for Christmas. But I will not get there. I never expected to be the one of us to go "over there" and fix the cabbageheads. When Ferd was passed by on account of his ear and you because of your operation I thought I was the lucky one but now I am not so sure. Remember Ferd answering Nature's Call in the woods and how the bumblebee flew in his ear and he could not get it out, his hands were elsewhere. It is funny now to think of it but it was not so at the time for poor old Ferd.

I have been riding a horse bareback and my butt is sore as a boil but it will get hard I guess. I am on guard tonight and will have to get a little sleep before going out. Before I close this letter I want to ask you if there are any of my old girlfriends around. I would like to see one of them. I would give her a good Christmas gift tonight. Ha, ha, ha.

Say, how is that kidney? Is it still bothering you or did it ever get well?

Now I will close. Hope I will hear from you soon and that you will have a good Christmas and a happy New Year. I remain

> Yours truly,
> Your old pal
> Bill

6   *the YMCA logo. a purple three-cent stamp. a Montgomery, Alabama, postmark.*

> Foreign Waters
> 12-30-17

Dear Brother,

Just a line to let you know I have not forgotten you. It was good to get your letter and to know that you do not feel hard toward me any more. You are right, that business is over and done with. I don't know what got me to thinking that way Joe, it must have been something I "et". Anyway I am glad it is all behind us. I hope you will find yourself a girl someday soon and settle down and never live alone again tho as you say they don't make many like Dot. Maybe then I will stop worrying.

Well, Joe, we are not allowed to write of where we are or how we came here so there is nothing much to write about. I am in good health and feel pretty good except for having plenty of stomach trouble but I guess we must expect that and take things as they come. I fell off the temperance wagon along with everybody else the night before we shipped out, I did not want to seem standoff-ish, but that was the only time. All I saw of New York

City was bars and fisticuffs. Out here I am not tempted,
it is easy to be sober on a ship. Take good care of yourself and be good from your brother

F. H. Hubbard
U.S.S. *Panther*

7   *a woven envelope the color of old money. a red two-
cent stamp. green notepaper. a fine penciled hand.*

Wheeling, W. Va.
June 21, 1918

Dear Friend:

I certainly was surprised to hear from you. I certainly
do appreciate your sympathy. I am glad somebody feels
sorry for me. I am also glad you have thought of me but
you know I love another and always will. I made my
choice and Joe, it is final. I have had one good man,
couldn't find any better no matter what others say. I never
expected to marry again. Mama and I have the restaurant
so I have got a way of making my living and therefore I
do not need any man. I am sorry to hear of your ill
health. I hope you will enjoy good health someday. I
never expect to look the same as I did when you last saw
me. It would be best for you and me too Joe if you forget
that silly young girl. I will close now with hope to hear
from you again. Frank Junior is playing with me, I can
hardly write.

Your friend,
Mrs. F. H. Hubbard

8   *the woven envelope. the two-cent stamp. the tiny hand.*

Wheeling, W. Va.
June 26, 1918

Dear Friend:

Got your letter and was as ever glad to hear from you.
I don't want you to think you offended me because you
didn't. I just neglected writing. I don't like to very much

any more. The picture you sent me was all right but your cheeks and lips were painted too much. Joe, I think you care more than you ought to. I am feeling lots better than I did. I think I will get my health back all right. But I do not expect to be happy. Just as you said, I have got lots to be thankful for, things could of been worse. My children are all well and as mean as they come. I hope this letter will revive you so you won't feel so bad. I don't like to see anybody that way. I have had my dish full. I hope you will excuse my scribbling because the children are bothering me. I will close

> With love,
> Mrs. F. H. Hubbard
> Answer soon.

9  *plain white paper. the tiny hand.*

> Wheeling, W. Va.
> July 2, 1918

Dear Friend:

Just a few lines to thank you for the book of Mrs. Eddy's. I am not sure it is for me though it may be for others. That is not for me to say. But I have seen too much of disease and dying up close to believe it is all in the mind. I was somewhat surprised to hear from you so soon. The children are well. Dorothy Mae will be 6 yrs. the twenty-eighth of this month. Frank Junior is 4 years old and Georgie will be 2 the 15th of August. Now you see Joe I have got quite a family. Well, take good care of yourself. I will close with

> Love,
> From your friend
> Mrs. F. H. Hubbard

10  *the woven envelope. the tiny hand. the penciled script.*

Wheeling, W. Va.
July 18, 1918

Dear Friend:

I got your letter and was glad to hear from you but sorry you were sick. I too have had a deep cold. All my children have too. I am sitting up in bed writing you. I am going to try to get up tomorrow. I am sorry to hear that you are having a hard time. You know that is all there is for some people in this world. You know it don't offend me for you to write. I love to read your letters. I can see that what you write you really mean. I don't see where you get that you are not good enough for me but man if you want a woman get one that hasn't got a family.

Answer soon,
From Dot
Mrs. F. H. Hubbard

11   *the tiny hand. the penciled script. the woven envelope.*

Wheeling, W. Va.
Aug. 7, 1918

Dear Friend:

Got your most welcome letter and as ever glad to hear from you. I am feeling much better and getting out a little. I am glad you are getting well and wish you the best of luck. When you are well and have got a car come over to see us. You certainly will be welcome. My people do not feel hard toward you the way you think, you are not Frank. Grandpa is not very well, he looks awful bad. Well, Joe, I have written so many letters today I am about to run out of steam. So I will close, hoping to hear from you soon

Yours respect.
Mrs. F. H. Hubbard

12    *blue-lined white paper. the small penciled script.*

Wheeling, W. Va.
Aug. 14, 1918

Dear Friend:

Your letter was rec'd. Was surprised to hear from you
so soon. You know I am always glad to hear from you. I
am sorry I couldn't attend Aunt Alma's funeral but you
know I have three to look after besides myself. My baby
has a bad cold. We all have been sick more or less all
summer. Mom is not feeling good. She has had the flu
like I have had it. So many have died here, it is hard to
go to one more funeral. I hope you are well and will get
along fine with your work. I have suffered two days with
toothache. I am going to have it pulled or fixed. That is
something I can't stand. Well, Joe, give the folks all my
best. We will all be glad when you come over. I will
close

With love,
From Dot

13    *buff paper with dark brown lines. the tiny hand. the
red two-cent stamp.*

Wheeling, W. Va.
Aug. 21, 1918

Mr. J. C. Hubbard:

Your letter rec'd. Was as ever glad to hear from you.
Also glad you are getting along fine with your work.
There is no work here yet but talk of the furnace starting
Monday. Some Union trouble which is delaying it. I am
glad you have recovered from the flu. It seems like a
person can hardly get rid of it. They say more have died
of it this year than ever before. My little ones are well
and this leaves me feeling nearly as good as new. You
ask me how my brother Howard is doing. He is working
in the mines when they run. Joe, I don't bother with
Howard very much. It seems all we do is quarrel. He is

so much like Papa. It drives him crazy that he cannot "lay down the law" to us the way Papa did, but I am sure that was how Papa meant it, since he left the restaurant to Mom and me, not to Howard. Joe, I have got the best Dr. in town working on my tooth. Thanks for your advice but it don't hurt anymore. Mom is better but not near well. She works the restaurant every day. Joe, please don't write about the time we fought in the summerhouse, that was long ago. I know I didn't have much sense then but I would like to give myself more credit than that now. You asked if I would have chosen different if I could have seen what Fate had in store. The answer is "I don't know." I wanted to leave Springfield which you could not or would not do. I was never happy there with everybody knowing my business and looking down their noses at a poor country girl, I thought I would explode and Joe, I look at it this way: If Mom had not sent me to Aunt Alma's to get citified I would not have met Frank and would not have my children who I could not live without, so it is just no use "supposing." Well I hope you will excuse my scribbling. Georgie hits my arms. I will close. Hope to hear from so dear a friend soon.

> Yours Respct.
> Dot

14    *the woven envelope. the tiny penciled hand.*

> Wheeling, W. Va.
> August 29, 1918

Dear Friend:

Your letter of a few days ago arrived. Am as ever glad to hear from an old friend. I am sorry to hear you have another cold. I know what they are to get rid of. Mom is still under the weather. I am worried about her, she talks funny at times. My health is good at present and my family is well. You ask why I have not sent a picture of myself. Joe, I did not get any letter asking for a picture.

It must have gone astray in the mails. I will ask the postman to look for it. Will see about having a picture made for you the next time there is someone through to make one, as I do not have any I like well enough to send. You also mentioned hearing something about my friend Ralph. Never pay attention to what people say Joe because people have got to talk, especially in Springfield, there is nothing else to do. It is true, Ralph is a prize fighter but he don't do much of it now, his heart is bad. And anyway he is living in Jackson, Mississippi. But don't let this worry you, he is not dangerous. I guess you will think this letter is punk but it is life. I am rather blue. I have heard people feel that way on their birthdays. You wonder where the time goes. It does not seem possible that I could be twenty-four, I do not feel it. If I remember right Joe you are six months older. Mom got up from her sickbed to make my cake although I told her not to. At my age you do not want to celebrate but we will have a nice ham and then angel cake if I can keep the children from running in the kitchen and from jumping on the floor while it bakes. Frank used to make my cakes fall on purpose. He said they tasted better that way. Joe, you ought to be glad you haven't nobody to worry about, only yourself. Children are certainly a worry but after a person has them they wouldn't part with them. You will see what I mean someday. Well Joe I will try to write a better letter the next time and will close with love

From,<br>Dot

15    *the woven envelope. the familiar penciled hand.*

Wheeling, W. Va.<br>Sept. 13, 1918

Dear Friend:

Your letter of a few days ago rec'd. Of course I was not angry that you forgot my birthday, I almost forgot it myself. Joe you should not take on so about it for there is no call to. You certainly are a good friend when it comes to cheering up old blue widows like me. Do you think I can ever pay you for being so nice to me when I have been so mean to you? Joe dear I have been careless about your feelings but will try from now on to be as nice as pie. I am feeling pretty good excepting a cold and I don't think I will ever get well of it. Dottie Mae is going to school now and likes it very much. I am glad that you are getting along fine with your work. I love to hear of you doing good. Mom, Howard, and Cliff are playing cards. Of course that is out of my line. I am pretty good at cooking and baking. Will try my hand for you when you come. Be sure your old Packard is in good shape, the roads are not like they are in Springfield. I don't know about you making a good Mamma, Joe, but maybe when the time comes you will make a good Papa. I will ring off because you will get tired of my scribbling.

> ans. soon
> I remain yours
> as ever,
> Dot

16  *the woven envelope. the tiny penciled hand.*

> Wheeling, W. Va.
> Sept. 20, 1918

Dearest Friend:

Your letter rec'd O.K. and as usual am glad to hear from such a dear. This leaves me and my family feeling fine. I am certainly sorry you had a bum operation but you know when a person has had an operation they never feel the same again. I have always thought you cared for me but not so much as that. Joe dear if you could get a nice girl and she would be good to you, you would never be lonely again. It is a hard job though to find the right kind. Please believe me when I say I am not the one, you must keep looking. I hope you will not think I am exaggerating, I mean just what I say. Well I hope these few lines will find you well. I will have to ring off for this time because I have another letter to write. Will try and write more the next time.

Ans. soon.
Yours as ever,
Dot

17  *the woven envelope. the red stamp. the tiny hand.*

Wheeling, W. Va.
Oct. 9, 1918

Dear Friend:
   Your letter rec'd. several days ago. You ask why I have not answered your last two letters. Joe, I did not receive two letters, only the one marked Oct. 4, which I am answering now. I always answer your letters as soon as I can. They must have got lost in the mails. You ask me who Cliff is. He goes with my mother and is a mighty good fellow. I have got so I play gin with them, they sure keep me knocking all the time. We have been cleaning house and painting and of course you know what that is. Mom is some better. Howard is working the restaurant with us, they never did open the mine. I know you will get sick of reading this scribbling so I will close

With love,
Dot
ans. soon

18  *the woven envelope. sepia ink. the tiny hand.*

Wheeling, W. Va.
Oct. 16, 1918

Dearest Friend:
   Your letter found me feeling better and not so blue. Gee Joe, I am cranky at times. I hope you will come soon and cheer me up. You are right, there are not many girls that want to settle down nowadays. I see you are

looking for the old fashioned kind. I am afraid they are hard to find. My children are well so far. The measles are thick around here now. This baby of mine sure is the limit. You ought to hear him talk. I hope you are well and getting along fine with your work. I don't mind the way you write, you are the same dear fellow you used to be. You will get tired of my scribbling so I will close with Love,

Dot

19  *the red stamp. the woven envelope. the tiny hand*

Wheeling, W. Va.<br>Oct. 29, 1918

Dearest Joe:
Your letter rec'd, as ever glad to hear from you. I am glad you have settled the question about coming. I certainly would like to see you. You know that you are welcome to come and see me where ever I am. I haven't found many men like you. Be sure and let me know what day you are coming so I can fix things and won't have to work much while you are here. The children are all well and this leaves me feeling pretty good. Mom is not feeling well. There is so much flu going around, I hope this is not what she's got. So Joe, hurry and get started. I might get tired of waiting. Well Joe, I have got another letter to write so I will close

With love,<br>as ever,<br>Dot

20  *the red stamp. an envelope with writing on the back in pencil: 'I have no use for the people that try to make it hard for us. Take it from me that your letter is O.K. and you are all right too.''*

Wheeling, W. Va.<br>Nov. 15, 1918

Dearest Joe:

Rec'd your letter of a few days ago. Was glad to hear you arrived home all right. I am awfully sorry Howard acted the way he did but you know there is always something to take the joy out of life. I think Howard lacks something in the upper story, and being out of work for so long has not improved his temper. You are a different man than Frank but Howard cannot see it or does not want to. Mom thinks you are a fine fellow. And so does Grandma. I certainly enjoyed going to the picture show with you even though the picture was sad, I do not like to think about the War. I thought with Mary Pickford in it, it would be a funny picture but it was not. Frank Junior is running around now. The measles didn't seem to hurt him much. I am glad you think I have got sweet children. I suppose it is because they come from such a sweet family, they are Hubbards. They are awfully mean at times, that comes from me. No Joe I was not disappointed in you. I thought maybe you would be in me, I am not getting any younger. I always try to be my old self but lots of times surroundings make me different. I get awful tired of quarreling with Howard. Sometimes your own people are worse to you than strangers. I am satisfied you think lots of me Joe and I certainly do appreciate it. I am sure glad you think more of me than to be foolish like some people in Springfield and believe what they say about me and poor Ralph. I have told you all there is to tell, and I know I can count on you to stick by me and believe me, and trust you to look at the bright side of things. Mom was awful sick after you left. I was worried about her. There was so much celebrating here on the Armistice that she got up and tried to help in the restaurant, but she was not strong enough and had to go home after 1 hour. I never saw so much drinking nor so many drunks. Well Joe dear I will ring off, you will get tired of my scribbling.

                                                  I will close
                                                  with my sincerest
                                                  love,
                                                  Dot

21   *the woven envelope. two green one-cent stamps.*

                                            Wheeling, W. Va.
                                            Nov. 20, 1918

Joe Hubbard:
    Your letter rec'd and am somewhat surprised at the
things you said. Guess you are more like other folks in
Springfield than I thought. Well it don't make any difference to me. I will never make no more explanations,
there is nothing to explain, and as far as people claiming
to be my friends I haven't any. There was never nothing
between us and Ralph is long gone as I have said. I sent
him away and do not want him back and I want to tell
you this, I don't consider anybody in Springfield any better than me and as far as people talking all they got to
do is keep their own dooryards clean. Now listen Joe
there is no man who does anything for me or gives me
anything, only Mom and I will stick to her irregardless.
She is as good as those that talk about her. She has
worked all her life and my God you would think she
deserved some happiness how ever it comes, tho there is
nothing wrong going on only friendship and anyway Cliff
would marry her today if his wife would give him the
divorce. Joe I thought you were pretty sensible but I guess
I will have to change my mind. I will raise my children
the best I can. It is a shame people won't let a poor
widow alone when she tries and wants to do right. Don't
look for me in Springfield because you won't see me. It
don't make any difference what you think of me. I am
always the same Dot, only with a little more temper. It
is up to you whether you want to come here again. I think
my mother is the best in the world and if you knew her
like I do you would think so too. I do not understand

what you meant about Howard. It is true he is blunt-spoke and even rude at times where I am concerned, but what could be more "normal" than a brother looking out for his sister when there is no other man to do so? Joe, I will always try and remember you as a good, sensible fellow and not a man that has lost his head.

I am Yours Respct.,
Mrs. F. H. Hubbard

22 *buff-colored paper. the tiny hand.*

Wheeling, W. Va.
Nov. 26, 1918

Dear Friend:

Your letter rec'd. Was sure glad you explained things. Joe I couldn't think you was the kind of man to listen to gossip. Since you have been so nice and quick about answering my hateful letter I will tell you a few things Mom told me about her talk with Howard. She told Howard she thought it would be nice if you and I got together again. Howard told Mom he wouldn't urge anything like that on. He said you wasn't the kind of man I wanted and he didn't think I was the kind you wanted. Mom told him you was a nice fellow and always had been with me. Howard said I did not need to get tied up with another Hubbard since blood always tells and who could say how you might turn out ten years down the line. No matter how steady you appeared to be now, you might end up in the gutter just like Frank, and anyway it was wrong for a man to take his brother's wife. But don't think for a minute that a thing he said weighed any with me. Like Mom told Howard, no man will ever be good enough for me as far as he is concerned, whoever I care for he will fight out of sheer cussedness. But you know Joe I have my children, and I always think of their welfare first. I have an awful mean temper and am afeared no man and I could ever agree. I do wish though you could get a woman that is good and would be the same with you so you would not be lonely. I have always thought well of you dear and do not want to think otherwise. I am sure glad you didn't mean any reference to Mom and Cliff because they are two good people. Mom is some better than what she was, though she is not full well. There is lots of flu here still. I hope you will not feel hard at me for telling you what Howard said. He has not been the same since Papa died and does not want anyone else to be happy either, he cannot stand to see it. I explained things to you Joe about me and Ralph and that is what made me sore, that you did not listen to me but to others. I think you should take my word, I have never told you a falsehood so far and you know how people in Springfield talk. There is nothing else to do in town in the winter, it is different here in the country. I have a long trip every morning and evening to keep me busy when I am not at work. I have to go milk. How would you like that twice a day? This leaves me and my children feeling pretty good. I will close with

> Love from
> Dot
> Mrs. F. H. Hubbard

23   *blue-lined paper. Christmas stamps.*

> Dec. 1, 1918

Dear Friend:

If you cannot read this letter of Mom's bring it with you when you come at Christmas and I will read it for you. I hate to give it to you because Mom can't spell or write very good. But I feel like it is yours and you are the one to have it.

> From Dorothy

*there is no other letter in the envelope.*

24-28   *2-cent stamps. Springfield, Ohio, postmarks. envelopes addressed in pencil to Mrs. F. H. Hubbard, Wheeling, W. Va. the words* RETURN TO

*SENDER printed in heavy black ink. official red stamps at the bottom. the word DECEASED. the envelopes without letters.*

29 *a postmark dated December 21, 1918, 3 p.m. an envelope addressed to Mrs. Harold Otwell, Sr., Wheeling, W. Va. RETURN TO SENDER printed in heavy black ink, an official red stamp at the bottom. the words MOVED, LEFT NO FORWARDING ADDRESS. the envelope without a letter.*

30 *unlined buff paper. the heavy penciled script with flourishes.*

> 802 E. Arcadia Ave.
> Glendale, California
> June 18, 1919

My Dear Friend:

Perhaps you have concluded that I have forgotten you, but such is not the case. The fact of the matter is that I suffered agony untold as the result of a broken hand which was caused by being kicked while cranking Mr. Ford's infernal machine and the hand is far from being well yet.

Boy, oh boy! You will never realize what we went through during the trip. Breakdowns, mishaps, and long delays due to bad roads cost us nine weeks time and about thirteen hundred dollars in cash money. We are certainly glad we didn't come over in the days of "49" or we would not have reached here about June 4th. Poor Viola said she never cooked as many flap jacks in all her born days. We even had them for my birthday dinner out on the desert due to the fact that we had run out of provisions and the big car was broken down and we had to wait until Ferd could go back to town, forty miles away, to get repairs and some eats. I never expected to take up the old "ball and chain" but now that I have I find it suits me, she is a good sport. But it was not much of a honeymoon. You should think about marrying too Joe, though I guess there are not many girls to speak of in "dear old Springfield."

And while we are on the subject of marrying, Ferd has been carrying on quite a correspondence with Dot. He began writing her right after Frank died and did not mention it to you for fear you might think it improper, but she has been a widow for over a year and things are progressing so rapidly between them that Ferd is trying to save up the money for her and the children to come out here on the train. She has not said "yes" yet but old Ferd thinks she will so I thought it would not hurt to tell you. Ferd is quite taken with her and I can't say that I blame him. Even I had a "crush" on her back in Springfield. Poor Ferd almost lost her because of Howard Otwell's interference. Howard did not want Ferd to succeed in his suit and intercepted or returned his letters without telling Dorothy, even going so far as to steal some rubber stamps from the Post Office to make it look as if Dot had gone away or died! Ferd of course did not believe it. He finally reached the Sheriff of Wheeling on the telephone and learned that Dot was alive and well, so we drove from Detroit to Wheeling on Xmas Eve and arrived just in time to see Howard Otwell dragged away by the police! The unfortunate man had gone completely around the bend and set fire to the family restaurant, which burned to the ground, and was on his way to do the same to the barn when he was caught and subdued. He is in the state asylum, probably for good. Dot found over a dozen letters when she packed up Howard's things. She has no idea what drove him to it. Doubtless you have heard this story before but now you have it from the horse's mouth. Ferd and I stayed in Wheeling for several weeks, then drove Dot and her family to Jackson, Mississippi. Dot said she could not bear to stay in Wheeling. You know how people talk. Her mother is still there and has remarried. She is Mrs. B. H. Clifford.

Well, old top, we are here and sorry to say we are far from being pleased with our new home, notwithstanding the fact that this is ideal country with plenty of eats growing all around you. We are having fresh vegetables right out of the garden daily and they are dirt cheap. Wages here are exceptionally good and clothing cheaper here than in Detroit but boy, oh boy! They certainly burn you up on the rent, as little two and three room houses rent from $60.00 to $75.00 per month, so after all is said and done conditions here are not much better than back home. So far I have not found anything to do though Ferd drove to Hollywood last week and got two days work as an extra on a Mabel Normand picture. His head is so swelled he barely talks to us now. We mean to go to Seattle, Washington, in the Spring. Maybe you can visit us there, old top. I certainly hope so.

Well as I have no more news of interest I will close by asking you to write real soon to

> Yours sincerely,
> Bill

31  *a square white envelope addressed to Mr. J. C. Hubbard, Springfield, Ohio. the address printed in pencil. the letters S.W.A.K. in red crayon on the flap of the envelope. blue-lined paper. a childish hand.*

> Portland, Oregon
> April 13, 1934

Dear Uncle Joe,

Thank you for the sweater. Mother tells me to say you should not do so much. Uncle Joe, how did you know my favorite color is pink? I wore it to school yesterday tho Mother said I should not, I should save it for Sunday but I could not help myself, it was so pretty, and everyone thought it was swell, it was worth her being mad tho I hope Y-O-U are not. I am sorry you could not come to the party, it was a good one.

Daddy is in Corvallis again, he could not find work in Portland. I wish he could find a job on the ground. He says he gets dizzy at the top of those trees, tho Mother says he is only funning. So do not write or send anything to this address but to General Delivery, Corvallis, where we will be when school lets out.

Mother asks me to tell you she is sorry she cannot write too, but she is tired from cooking all day in the cafeteria then coming home and doing the same for us. My cooking is not so good Uncle Joe, but when you come to visit, I will make angel cake. Mother says it is your favorite. Love from your niece,

Ferdinanda

# Kismet

Brett found out first. Her boyfriend, Warren, who'd proposed after three years, insisted they take the AIDS test.

"Why not?" she said nonchalantly. Two weeks later, she knew why not. Brett tested HIV-positive, though she wasn't sick yet. Her immune system was still healthy, normal. Warren, who tested negative, left her immediately.

"That scumbag. That pig," she said of Warren, two hours into her telephone conversation with Jake, her first lover and best friend, who had first screamed at her, then comforted her, then forgiven her everything, as she forgave him, completely and sincerely, assuming—as they both did—there was something to forgive.

"He's always been a scumbag, sweetie. He's always been a pig. Most likely he always will be."

"I guess." Brett struck a match, lit a cigarette, took a long draw, and exhaled as she spoke. "But I never thought he'd be a pig to *me*. You know?"

"Of course I do."

"It's one thing to live with someone, I guess," she said. "It's another thing to die with them."

"Isn't it," he said.

Jake decided he should be tested too, though he thought

he knew what the results would be. He and Brett had made love a thousand times, twice a day when they lived together. He had tasted her blood. In the early eighties, they had shot drugs together. If Brett had the virus, Jake thought he had it too.

Jake didn't get tested in Fort Worth, where he lived. His family doctor played golf with his uncle, and Jake had dated a nurse once. He knew how they gossiped. He drove to a clinic in Dallas, where they gave his blood a number.

They were both writers, but neither were prodigies. In their mid-thirties, she had just begun to be published; he had just begun to win grants and prizes. She wrote about the dwindling fast lanes of Europe and America, where she felt at home. He wrote about his neighborhood in south Fort Worth. In the center of his literary world was the house he had been born in, had lived in all his life, and would probably die in, far sooner than expected.

Jake and Brett were not their real names, though few people remembered what their real names were. They had gone through twelve grades together. Jake fought Brett's schoolyard battles, protected her from bullies far and wide. At fifteen, they'd lost their virginity together, read Hemingway, and renamed each other. She had fallen in love with Lady Ashley at one sitting, then declared, in his arms, that he was very like Jake Barnes.

"Why?" he'd asked in her father's Lincoln, taking her hand and putting it on him proudly. "Nothing's wrong with *me*."

"His equipment was damaged, true. But so is yours." She had moved her hand, drawn a heart on his chest with her finger. "You love me, right? But you don't really love me. Not head over heels."

At thirteen, he had watched both his parents die: first his father of a heart attack; then his mother, who had withered away from grief. They had been so in love. They had not even been forty. It was a persistent source of pain for Jake that, after his father died, he hadn't been enough for his mother to live for. His mother and father had been head over heels. Jake swore he never would be.

But Brett, at fifteen, had been rich and beautiful. Her parents had given her everything, always; why wouldn't Jake? "Maybe you'll change your mind," she had said, stroking his hairless chest, unwilling to admit to failure so early.

"I'll *never* change," he had said firmly. Their whole lives were built on this interchange. Brett had tried to change his mind, but Jake had never changed it, had never given the love she'd tried so hard to wrest from him. He'd never budged, though at times he'd wanted to, and his obstinacy enraged her. They'd lived together several times, had once been formally engaged. But Jake had never loved her enough. He'd always pushed her away. Brett had always tried to make him jealous, but he'd never once been jealous. Finally, she'd gone to New York, had come back to Texas six months later, then gone away a second time for good, more or less. Jake stayed put and waited for her visits. He was always there for her, up to a point.

Jake loved to live alone, but Brett didn't. While their friends married, produced children, bought real estate and cats, Brett went from man to man without stopping. Their friends loved her exploits and recounted every new episode with poorly disguised glee.

"Everything's so boring these days," they would say. "No one has any fun."

"Well . . . there's Brett. The madcap heiress."

In the creek across the street from his house, where Jake used to fish for crawdads, lived millions of tiny insects known as skitterbugs. They move so fast you can't even see them, only the trails they make on the water.

Brett was a skitterbug. She bisected her own path. And when she dared Jake to dive off the high board at Forest Park pool, or to swim from a boat in the deepest part of Eagle Mountain Lake, when she beckoned him from the water like Circe in a white bikini, dared and jeered and splashed him, Jake would look at her fondly and then say this: "I'm not afraid of the water. I'm afraid of what's *in* it."

Brett and Jake should have married, probably. But Jake wouldn't change. He wouldn't be pushed. Eventually, Brett had slowed down, landed. She had found Warren. It hadn't been perfect, but it had been something. Though she had still flirted, just to keep her hand in, Warren had always been acceptably jealous. He'd kept her under control. She'd gotten a lot of work done. When Jake got his test results back in June—positive, as he knew they would be—he wished that he and Brett had married. He wished that, long ago, they'd given up, compromised, and settled for each other.

On the telephone, they talked about where they'd gotten the virus. Brett favored Martine, a French junkie of whom Jake had once been enamored, who had introduced him to the dubious joys of speedballing. It was hard to be a junkie in Texas, but Jake, inspired by Brett, had managed it for a year or so. After Martine, there was an English nurse, who stole clinical morphine from John Peter Smith Hospital, where she worked. (It wasn't really being a junkie, Ruth had said, as long as you only shot up between your toes, like they did.) When Ruth had gotten caught and deported, Jake flushed the rest of the morphine down the toilet, then called Brett to tell her about it.

"What a waste, baby," Brett had said. "You could've sent it to me." Brett loved opiates. When she started using drugs, she went straight to heroin with no intermediate stops. Everything else was for sissies, she said.

"Myself? Only *more* so?" Brett would say when some

...ing egomaniac offered her cocaine. She wanted to escape her thoughts, not revel in them. Heroin gave her that. It was healthier too, or so she said. "Have you ever seen an old coke fiend?" she'd say. "I mean, *chronologically* old?" Jake would admit he hadn't.

Brett loved to sit in Village bars and talk to the old junkies, the hipsters, the jazzmen. She loved to listen to their stories about William Burroughs and Jack Kerouac, then shoot up with them in Lower East Side hovels or take them to their methadone clinics in cabs. She loved shooting up with rock stars and actors too, and none of it ever seemed to hurt her. She'd carried her works in a jewel case from Tiffany's, before a few of her famous new friends OD'd.

"They'd have it now too, if they weren't already dead," Brett said of the late Sid Vicious and Nancy Spungen, with whom she'd often shot up. Their deaths had shaken her badly. Also, she'd been afraid of losing her money, the bulk of which she'd finally inherited. Heroin, she said, was poverty in a syringe. Jake had talked her into checking into Hazeldon by letting it drop that Marianne Faithfull was there. Brett had been clean ever since, though she complained about it often. She didn't see the point. She missed her drugs.

Brett said, "Oh, baby. I hate him so much." Jake knew she was talking about Warren. "Because I have it and he doesn't. Is that a stupid reason to hate someone?"

"That's not why you hate him. You hate him because he dumped you when you needed him most. You *should* hate him. He's a little shit."

"I guess I loved him, at one point."

"You never loved him."

"No," she agreed. Warren was an arbitrageur, a close personal friend of Ivan Boesky. Brett thought—*hoped*—he would soon be in jail.

"The only person you ever loved was me," Jake said.

"That's right."

"So when are you coming home?"

"Do you mean that?"

"Of course I do. You shouldn't be alone now. Neither should I."

"But baby, don't you think it's time you got the hell out of Texas?" Jake had never been out of Texas, except to go south, into Mexico, to hunt.

"Why?" he said. Because I might not get another chance, he thought.

"It's so hot in Texas, in the summer," Brett said.

"As you know, there's air conditioning."

"I have this cute little house, right off the beach. There's a garden, and flowers, and butterflies, and tame Bambis, and all sorts of birds—"

"Remind me to pack my gun," he said.

"—and two flop-eared bunnies, morning and night. They used to be pets, I guess, but somebody dumped them." Warren had exiled her to Fire Island, had promised to come on weekends. But Warren never came. "The rent's paid until September fifteenth. It's small, but we could turn both bedrooms into offices and sleep on the couch."

"All right," he said, surprising them both. "In September, we'll go back to Texas."

A week later he'd shown up in Kismet with his bags. She met him at the dock with her little red wagon. She was wearing, over a bright blue bathing suit, a T-shirt Jake recognized. It had belonged to an old boyfriend of hers, a friend of Jake's, a poet. Jake wondered, idly, about the poet's health.

Before he kissed her, he fingered the T-shirt, which irritated him, although he didn't know why. "Don't you have anything of your own?" he said crossly. Brett stripped off the T-shirt and threw it into the bay.

"I have you," she said, then put her arms around him and cried. "That's the first time in our lives you've ever been jealous."

"I'm not jealous," he said.

"And over Perry Wentzel's T-shirt! If I'd known, I'd have worn it *years* ago."

"I don't have a jealous bone in my body," he said.

Brett's cottage, on Seabay Walk, was sweet and tiny. The garden was lush. In addition to the bees and flop-eared bunnies, which Brett had already tired of, after one too many bouts of cleaning flop-eared bunny shit, there were frogs, crickets, beetles, flies, spiders, moths, and snakes. Brett had rented a computer for Jake, like the one he had in Texas. His office was small, but clean and light. The ocean was over a dune. It wasn't home, but it was fine. It was theirs. It was better than home.

In Kismet, the writer's block that had afflicted them both melted like fog in the sun. They worked hard in their offices. They read to each other. They had never been so productive.

Every day they walked at least five miles. Brett had sent away for stacks of pamphlets on how to bolster their immune systems, though both of them were symptom-less. Maybe they always *would* be, Brett's doctor had said, after analyzing their blood. Their T-cell counts were normal. Their immune systems were strong. Their bodies could still fight off disease. But with AIDS, nothing was certain. So exercise was highly recommended, along with a fresh, whole diet. Brett ordered produce from the King Kullen in Bayshore and cooked their meals from a macrobiotic cookbook.

They became vegetarians, ate vitamins by the handful. They had decided not to try any drugs, since none of them had been proved to help the symptomless, but every morning, Brett made a home version of AL 721, a food supplement that might or might not strengthen the walls of their cells, in the blender. She mixed soy lecithin with fresh orange juice and melted butter. It tasted like an Orange Julius.

After a month, their tongues were coated. Their faces began to break out. They were sure they were starting to die. But the volunteer manning the Gay Men's Health Crisis hotline which they finally reached after six embarrassed hang-ups explained that they weren't dying quite yet. A macrobiotic diet often had that effect, he said with the kindest voice in the world, a voice that made Brett cry. Their bodies were trying to heal by secreting poisons. Brett's doctor, when they saw him, told them the same thing. He told them to *hope*. For the first time in his life, Jake was glad of Brett's money. The doctor's visits were expensive. Neither of them had insurance.

Several weeks later, their bodies adjusted. Their tongues pinkened. The rashes stopped. Both of them firmed up, lost weight, and got tans at the nude beach in front of the old Kismet lighthouse, where the only people who took off all their clothes were elderly men. They reminded Jake of the stuffed frogs sold down in Mexico, standing on their hind legs, tummies protruding, playing mariachis and wearing funny hats. The fat naked frogmen in Kismet wore watches. Some of them smoked pipes and read *The New York Times*. Jake found it difficult not to stare at their penises.

Brett and Jake stopped drinking, but Brett refused to stop going to bars. Every weeknight, they went to the Kismet Inn, where they played pinball, drank club soda, watched *Jeopardy* and *Hollywood Squares*, and talked to the fishermen and carpenters. They seldom went out during the weekends. From their new positions as casualties, the pickup scene was difficult to take. Every day that summer there were stories in the papers about AIDS, so many that Brett and Jake had stopped reading the papers, but the warnings didn't seem to be having much effect.

"It doesn't seem to be sinking in, does it?" Jake said, the first Friday night they went to the Inn. "I Want Your Sex" was on the jukebox.

"Not much. It doesn't seem to be slowing them down."

"Fiddling while Rome burns?"

"I guess," she said.

Middle-aged morticians and pharmacists buzzed around Brett like honeybees, bragging about their dough-re-me while knocking back strange-colored drinks. Computer programmers and contractors offered her boats and condominiums, got surly when she wouldn't play ball, while ridiculing the women who did. When Brett mentioned a woman she'd rented a house from once, a bartender said, "Was that before or after she put the revolving door on her bedroom?"

"That's a bitch, there," one of the men, old and pot-bellied, said of Brett one night, after she'd taken his hand off her leg for the third or fourth time.

"Because I hate being felt up in bars?" she said.

Later, another man said this: "I hear your body is your temple, baby. Can I worship there too?"

Total strangers complimented her breasts, as if they were clothing. Brett once turned to Jake and said of the Oakdale electronics czar who was trying to woo her, "Just imagine, baby. Not only is his *boat* bigger than yours, so is his *swimming pool*."

The rejected suitor stood up. "Well, pardon me for living. Just pardon me," he said.

"I probably shouldn't make fun of them," Brett said, after the man had gone.

Jake said, "Why not?" He had no sympathy for anybody healthy.

"Oh, you know. Fish in a barrel?"

"I guess," said Jake. A new man sat down next to Brett and smiled at her hopefully. ACCOUNTANTS NEED LOVE TOO, his T-shirt read.

Jake wasn't used to being jealous. He didn't know whether to be proud or angry when he watched the men watch Brett. Every night they were propositioned, separately or together. (They looked so much alike, small and lean and dark, green-eyed, that people thought they were brother and sister, an added lure for the kinky.) There was always a new hot tub to go to. Brett called them "AIDS distribution centers." And though they found a used condom once, on Seabay Walk, they doubted that safe sex was in the Kismet dictionary. It was still an oxymoron, like French rock and roll.

Once somebody told a joke about AIDS, in which two Polish junkies, sharing a needle, met a friend's admonition with the line, "It's okay, we're wearing condoms!" Everybody at the bar roared. Jake wanted to get up and scream, Hey, assholes! It's no fucking joke! It was a good thing Jake wasn't drinking, or he might have. Brett took one look and got him out right away. They stopped going to the bars on weekends.

"This is where Margaret Fuller died," Brett said, the day they walked to Point O'Woods.

"Don't be morbid," Jake said. "It's bad for your health." He had read the pamphlets too, all of them, from cover to cover, though he had never let Brett see him do so.

"I'm not being morbid, baby. I'm just pointing it out. I read all about it. She came back from Europe, all married up, with her Italian husband and sprout, and everything was fine until she got right out there . . ." Brett pointed to the ocean and paused dramatically.

"And then?"

"They brought all this marble back from Italy," Brett said, her voice low and full of relish. "These statues. I don't know what for. They were in the hold of the ship and somehow they got untied and started slipping around and one of them rammed a hole through the boat. *Finito*."

"You're kidding," he said.

"Uh-uh. I read it in the encyclopedia. It happened just that way. Instead of the ship hitting a rock or something, it came apart from the inside out."

"And everyone died?"

"Nope. Only the rich and famous."

"That must be what they call *submersive* art," he said expectantly. Jake was addicted to bad puns. Brett smiled sweetly and took his arm.

"Do you think we'll be in the encyclopedia, baby?"

"Not likely," he said, then noticed her sad face. "Maybe. If we work hard, if we're lucky—"

"Not likely."

"—we'll be in the encyclopedia," he continued. "Someday. Maybe. It's possible." If we live long enough, he thought, but didn't say.

Brett smiled. She had always wanted to be immortal, to be in the encyclopedia. She wanted people who didn't know her to remember her name. Jake wanted this too, just as much as Brett did.

In Weatherford, where Jake's father was born and his grandparents still lived, there was a statue of Mary Martin in her Peter Pan costume. Mary Martin had been Weatherford's most famous citizen, until her son, Larry Hagman, got famous too, and Jim Wright became Speaker of the House, but nobody built statues of them. Mary Martin's statue was in Cherry Park, where Jake had played. When Jake got tired of the swings and tiltywhirl, he would sit under it and think about being famous. He wasn't sure how he would get to be famous, or for what, but he knew it would happen. (The sun is hot in Texas in the summer. Maybe the heat had fried his brains.) Jake had told Brett about the statue and his dreams the first night they made love.

One day when the temperature was a hundred and three, when Brett was in Texas healing from some affair gone bad, they'd driven to Weatherford to see Mary Martin's statue. Jake couldn't find it. He and Brett had walked all over Cherry Park, looking for it. Had he *dreamed* it?

Jake had called his grandmother, pretending to be in Fort Worth. He hadn't wanted to visit his grandparents, because Brett had been with him, and his grandparents had never liked her, though Brett didn't know this. She couldn't imagine anybody not liking her, but Jake's grandmother thought she was fast. His grandfather said she put on airs. Because Brett was rich and Jake wasn't, his grandparents had never trusted her, but Jake never told Brett this. His grandparents never let on either. They were courteous to the bone.

When Jake visited his grandparents, they always went to the cemetery. His grandmother would put on her sunbonnet, get down on her knees, and pull the weeds around his parents' graves. She would complain about the groundskeepers. She would say to Jake, as she had said many times before, "There's always a place for you here, honey, if you need it." Jake had lied to his grandmother to avoid that cemetery visit. She'd been happy to hear from him. He'd worked the conversation around to Mary Martin's statue, finally.

"Lawsy!" his grandmother had said. "What made you remember that old thang?" Jake had said something lame. "Somebody stole it, honey," his grandmother had gone on. "Kids, most likely. Back aways. Why, it must've been ten years! On Halloween. But the base is still there, that the statue set on."

Walking back to Kismet, Jake thought about Mary Martin, who'd had a long, full life. She was old and gray, but still singing, *still alive*. Mary Martin would be in the encyclopedia, but he and Brett wouldn't, except as part of a roster of unfulfilled promise, black-bordered, chiseled on granite somewhere maybe, a roundup of those who, at the end of the century, had died young.

When they got home, Jake wrote this in his journal: *There will never be a statue of me in Cherry Park. Little boys will never sit under it dreaming. Not of me.*

Two hours later, Brett saw the bruises.

"Come in here, baby," she called from the bathroom. "Please come quick. I need you."

Jake got up from his desk, heart pounding, and walked

into the bathroom. Brett was standing in front of the mirror, trying to examine her backside.

"Were these here yesterday?" she said, pointing to an ugly line of bruises on her left hip.

"I don't know," he lied. He had noticed the bruises a week ago. They hadn't faded at all.

"Baby . . ." she said and started to cry. There were some things from which he just could not protect her. He put the toilet seat down and sat on it, took her hand, and pulled her toward him. There were more bruises underneath her rib cage, but Brett hadn't noticed those yet.

"You've always bruised so easily," he said.

"Horse shit."

"You've always had sensitive skin. Don't you remember?"

"I don't know my body anymore. It's not mine. I don't recognize it."

"You have such beautiful skin," he said, touching it lightly.

"I don't inhabit it. I don't know who's in here. I feel like some kind of knock-knock joke."

Jake kissed the bruises.

"What's this?" Brett said, pointing to a tiny spot.

"That's a freckle, sweetie."

"Are you sure?"

"We're in the sun all day. You've always freckled."

"Was this there before?" she said, pointing to a small mole, which he also kissed.

"It's always been there."

"Are you sure? What about that one?"

"It's a mole too."

"I never noticed it," she said. Her voice was rising dangerously.

"Hush now."

"Are my glands swollen?" Brett stroked her pretty throat.

"If they are, it's because you poke them all day."

"I don't," she said, but she did, unconsciously, while talking on the phone or reading. Jake did the same thing, but by himself, alone, in the bathroom.

They noticed someone else doing it too, a lawyer friend of Brett's who came to visit. They were finishing their dinners at the Inn, when Brett and Jake saw him stroke his throat absentmindedly, like some men stroke their beards. Brett looked around quickly. No one else had noticed, or if they had, they didn't understand. She reached across the table and stopped the hand in mid-stroke. The lawyer blanched. His eyes met Brett's, then Jake's, then Brett's again, in recognition. She held his gaze for the longest time. The lawyer burst into tears. They paid the check and took him home. The three of them talked all night. It felt good to talk about it, Jake thought, to somebody else besides Brett.

"You were wonderful," he'd told her in bed that morning.

"It's easy to be brave, for somebody else," she'd said.

So far, no one but Warren, and now the lawyer, Jeffrey, knew about it. Brett was sure Warren wouldn't blab, at least not for the six months it would take for him to find out whether he was positive himself. Warren was a Jew. He was sure they were building concentration camps.

"In six months, if he's negative, we'll be fair game. He'll tell *everybody*," she said.

"We'll worry about that in six months."

"I feel sorry for him, actually."

"I don't," Jake said.

They talked about telling their old lovers. They argued about who could take it and who couldn't, about whose lives would end with the news, figuratively or literally, about which of them would take the test or simply worry themselves to death, about who would change their behavior or hurl themselves at enemies like javelins. They thought about sending anonymous letters, since there were a number of their lovers they did not wish to speak to. Finally they did nothing, told no one. They didn't risk exposing themselves. They didn't save a single life.

During these conversations, Jake realized he didn't remember the names of all his old girlfriends, or whatever the women he'd slept with had been. He was sure he'd known all their names at some point. It embarrassed him to admit this lapse to Brett.

"You've always been a slut," she said happily. Jake seldom admitted to any faults at all. She loved it when he said, as he almost never did, that he was wrong. "From the first, you were easy as pie."

Jeffrey had suggested that they marry before the test became compulsory and things tightened up, as he put it. Late in August, they obtained insurance fraudulently. The doctors spent less than twenty minutes on their examinations. They made wills, leaving everything to each other. They were married in Bayshore, twenty years from the day they'd first made love.

After the wedding, they went into the nearest bar as one, downed two tequilas each without speaking, then remembered, when the liquor hit, that they shouldn't be drinking.

"Oh, dear," Brett said, holding up her shot glass.

"Look what we've done," Jake said.

"Oh, dear. Our poor systems." Brett giggled.

"Let's have another drink." Jake signaled for the bartender.

"Only if you'll take me dancing later."

"All right," he said.

Later, after they'd danced, taken a water taxi to Kismet, and made love, Brett said, "I never thought I'd do well as an old person." Brett had always romanticized death. She saw herself in the bull ring instead of in the stands, clutching a severed ear in her handkerchief. She thought she was Jimi Hendrix or Janis Joplin. She would live fast, die young, and leave a beautiful corpse. She thought that justified the books they'd never write, the children they'd never have, the people they'd never be. But Jake had seen the photographs. The corpses were not beautiful.

"No. Neither did I," he lied. In fact he'd always pictured himself old, white-haired and robust like his grandfather, sitting on his front porch in Texas, whittling sticks into puppets for somebody else's children. He'd pictured himself alone. Always.

He turned on the light and got out of bed to go to the bathroom. He looked in the mirror, stretched his neck, and felt his glands, but he couldn't see any change. He couldn't feel any swelling.

When he turned off the light in the bathroom, it was almost dawn. He heard a sound on the patio he didn't recognize, like a squeaky hinge. He went outside. Cliff swallows had built a nest under the roof deck. The eggs had hatched. Little heads were sticking their necks out, screaming for food.

Jake closed the patio door softly, trying not to disturb the birds. When he went back into the bedroom, Brett had turned over. The sheet had slipped off her. Her backside was covered with purple bruises.

Jake turned off the light, pulled the shades, and got into bed. In the dark, he kissed the bruises he could no longer see.

"I love you, Sue Ann," he said. The name sounded strange when he'd said it, during the ceremony. Now it sounded just right.

"Oh, I know," she said happily. She chuckled, deep in her throat. It was a wonderful sound, he thought. "This was some day, wasn't it, Billy?"

"It was," he said. "It certainly was." He pulled her close and started to cry.

That night, in his dreams, he stood on top of a grassy hill. He looked down and saw Brett, still damp from the lake, naked and beautiful, unmarred, laughing, calling to him. Jake crouched down and put his arms around his knees. His Levi's were white. He worried about grass stains. Then Brett held her arms out. Jake tucked in his head. He let go. He tumbled. He fell.